DEMONS

Darkness Series #4

K.F. BREENE

Copyright © 2014 by K.F. Breene

All rights reserved. The people, places and situations contained in this ebook are figments of the author's imagination and in no way reflect real or true events.

✾ Created with Vellum

SYNOPSIS

It's been a long road, but Sasha has finally claimed her role as the least knowledge mage in history. She's also acquired a new, incredibly grumpy bodyguard, and a spunky new BFF. With her team by her side, she learns the ropes of this new profession.

Her experience level is about to be fast-tracked, however.

On a routine trip to check out a perimeter breach, she encounters a hideous demon called by an experienced magic worker. It is this terrifying discovery that unlocks a deeper problem: Stefan's troubled past and the reason he gravely mistrusts the Mata.

While Sasha struggles to fight the physical demons, Stefan struggles to fight the demons of his past. If he fails, his future in Sasha will be lost.

CHAPTER ONE

"Um...hi." I inched into the dimly lit room wearing a black pant suit that denoted my status as the least knowledgeable mage in history. Dominicous and Toa waited for me patiently, Dominicous with his ankle crossed over his knee, and Toa displaying great posture.

This was one of the rooms that needed extensive repairs after the first battle I'd ever experienced. Once the dust had settled, most of the front of the house, and a great portion of the back, lay in tatters from enemy magic blasting. The interior had been rebuilt, as well as updated, and now the room dripped refinement and elegance for which Stefan's clan—and my clan, too—was known.

The renovation didn't make this meeting any more comfortable.

"Sasha, yes. Please," Dominicous pointed to the chair in front of him, "have a seat."

"Okay."

I entered the rest of the way into the room, closing the door behind me. Toa had that flat, blue-eyed stare going. It was amazing that I still hadn't gotten used to it. Although, in my defense, a nonblinking eye rape was rarely the kind of thing you just eased into.

After I was seated, I looked expectantly from one man to the other, waiting to find out why I was summoned.

Dominicous started. "There are a few things I'd like to discuss. The first, and most unusual, concerns our history. I'm sure Stefan has told you the nature of my personal interest in you?"

I gulped, sweat starting under my arms. He was talking about when I was five years old and got in a really bad car accident. My entire family had been killed, along with people in four other cars. I had been the sole survivor. Not only that, but I ended up a mile away, sitting in a park on my own, with little more than second-degree burns and a bad gash to the head.

Apparently Dominicous was the reason I ended up there, having plucked me out of the aftermath of the wreckage and moved me a safe distance away. He'd also given me blood. From his vein. Kind of gross.

"He has, no doubt, also told you," Dominicous went on, "that it appears I will not be able to have children. I have tried for..." His face fell, briefly, before he composed himself again. "Decades. Which puts us in a unique situation. You have no parents or family to speak of. I have no heir. We both find ourselves in the same world with similar experiences, regardless of which race we were originally born into. The outcome is obvious; I would like to formally adopt you."

My breath exited my body in a ragged *whoosh*. While I'd had a foster family since I was seven, they'd never adopted me. They'd taken the state funds for orphans and allowed me to reside within their house until I was old enough to move on. And while I was extremely lucky to have ended up with loving foster parents and their normal, bratty children, I'd always been different. Not outcast, but separate. Soulwrenchingly alone. That fact had left me unable to thoroughly trust anyone, and nowhere to put down roots.

So to sit in this chair, in a job I didn't know how to do properly, in a world I hardly fit into, and to have someone ask to adopt me even though I was a pain in the ass... I couldn't stop the tears from raiding my eyes.

"But, am I too old to adopt? I'm twenty-two." I gave him a watery grimace. I probably didn't have to mention that I acted nowhere near my age.

"Being that I don't exist in the human records, that isn't a concern of mine. You will be adopted in our way, which is to say, welcomed into my family hearth and signed onto my documents as an heir. I'm sure you realize that with multiple partners, we don't always know the fathers of children. It is why we set up a hearth with our mate, welcoming any children she has or begets."

"But—and I'm just trying to understand, here—but can't you just snag a woman that already has a kid? Rather than open yourself to jokes and snide remarks because I'm human... "

"I can, yes. I had a mate long ago, but she died. I was working toward that path again when you resurfaced in my life. It seems you are deeply entwined with Fate. And me with you. There is a reason you survived that horrible accident. And a reason I was nearby to pluck you out. While I do not know that reason, I don't turn my back on the divine, and being that you are more my child than any I would claim through mating, this solves my problem nicely. And yours.

"You would gain a family and a dowry. From me, you would bring status and political influence to your chosen mate. From you...I would finally have the stability only a family can provide. Your magic would disband any naysayers, and Stefan's mark would further silence them. There will always be prejudice, of course—that can't be helped, as you know—but it would be lessened with both your magic and my influence. I think this would work out in the best ways for both of us."

All I could do was blink at him for a few minutes. While it sounded more like a business proposition than anything, his eyes had gone soft and a comforting smile I'd never seen before played around his lips. He wanted me in his family. Me: idiot human with a ton of power and absolutely no sense.

Through the warm gush in my middle, I found my voice enough to say, "Wow. That's pretty thought-out."

Dominicous' smile grew. "In my position, something of this magnitude cannot be entered into lightly. Plus, I'm fond of you. It was emotion that led me to take you from the wreckage in the first place. This is the right decision. I feel it."

Another few tears slipped down my cheeks. I nodded, not really knowing what to say.

Dominicous' eyes twinkled. "Good. That's settled then. Plus, you're human. I'll get grandchildren."

"Which will turn your hair white from stress, I'm sure," Toa added in a dry voice.

I rolled my eyes at Toa; he was just pissed he couldn't unravel half the weird magical spells I accidently created.

"Wonderful. Let's continue," Dominicous said, more chipper than I'd ever seen him. "We plan to take a trip back to the council. We have Trek, the white mage from the Eastern Territory, who needs to be brought in. We plan to use him as proof an uprising is occurring. The lead council member has taken a mental hiatus—we need to pull him back into leadership. As a new mage of high magical status, you are also required to give your due. We will need to bring you into the fold. How is your leg?"

I looked down at my scrawny shin, newly out of the cast. "It's okay. A bit weak."

"Yes, that is to be expected. And how is your relationship with the *Mata?* Strong as ever, I hope?"

The *Mata* were Shape Changers. I'd fought beside them in the last battle in which we captured Trek, the caped idiot. I'd been given Pack Friend status on a kinship level, which meant I was someone they would fight beside if it ever came up. It was kind of a big deal.

"It's good, except...well, Stefan isn't thrilled when I go to see them," I admitted.

That was an understatement! Stefan nearly foamed at the mouth every time I so much as mentioned Tim, the alpha. God forbid I try to go visit without both Charles and Jonas at my back. His behavior was ridiculously overprotective, for no discernible reason. Whenever I tried to talk about it, his mouth got as thin as his patience.

Toa blinked. Which meant he knew something!

I jumped on it immediately. "What am I missing? What's Stefan's problem with them?"

Toa glanced at Dominicous, whose gaze bored into mine. "He has history with the *Mata*. It is not for me to discuss."

I felt my eyebrows dip. Stefan generally told me everything, both about his feelings—which he usually hated admitting—or anything relevant to the clan. As mage, and hopefully co-leader one day, I needed all relevant information to make informed decisions.

Or so Jonas constantly told me. I barely had hold of my magic, and now I was supposed to learn how to lead. Needless to say, the pressure was mounting, one mountain at a time.

"Interesting," I muttered, biting my lip.

"You see? She has an unhealthy amount of curiosity and nosiness," Toa reflected.

"I don't point out your flaws of stubbornness and sulkiness, do I?" I shot back.

Toa sniffed. "Yes, you do..."

Dominicous laughed. "Okay, Sasha, go create havoc. We'll meet again in a week or so to discuss our visit to the council. We have some time, yet. A few representatives from the *Mata* will be accompanying us, so hopefully you can smooth the working relationship between Stefan and their alpha in the meantime."

Fat chance. They each wanted to bash the other's head in. Tim tried for patience, and usually then tried not to pick up something heavy and swing it in Stefan's direction. Stefan tried not to growl and bluster and bodily pick Tim up and throw the bear shifter out of the mansion. Pretty much the best they could each do was stare, flex, and wish I didn't have any interaction with the other.

It wasn't a recipe for a lovely afternoon picnic.

I was nearly skipping out the door when I met the frosty stare of one of my bodyguards.

"What are you so happy about, human?" Jonas asked, pushing forward from the wall.

Jonas didn't like me personally, and he didn't like that I was human, but because his brain had made the connection that I was not only necessary to the well-being of his clan, but also important, he'd assigned himself the role of my protector. He would, and had, laid down his life to keep me alive.

I think he hated himself more than me.

And yes, normal people would reciprocate that hate—the guy had left me for dead the first time we'd come in contact with each other. Plus, he was a vicious, grumpy a-hole. But for all that, he did save me from capture, and Stefan had implicit trust in him. Plus, I was terrible at holding a grudge, and the guy was hilarious if you took him with a grain of salt.

To that end, I flashed him a huge smile and said, "Dominicous is adopting me!"

Jonas snorted. "Only a fool would tie himself to you."

"You just called yourself a fool."

"That's different."

"You called Stefan a fool, too."

Jonas' eyebrows dipped low over his eyes, his customary irritated look. "We have a possible territory breach at the West Third. Also, your furry friends are here. They say two of theirs went missing around that area, so they want to come along. The Boss says no, but it's your expedition because he's tied up, so it's your call."

"Obviously I'm going to say they can come."

Jonas yanked the door open leading into the front greeting room and impatiently gestured me through. He was a gentleman at heart—another trait he hated about himself.

"They're not riding with me. I don't want to have to flea bomb my car," he said when we were within hearing range.

"Would it kill you to be nice?"

"Yes."

Tim fell silent as I came in sight and turned to me expectantly. Being in his late twenties, Tim was the youngest alpha for his pack in nearly fifty years. The fact that he led a giant, North American faction made him an anomaly. He'd gotten the title the same way Stefan had gotten his leadership role, by fighting for it. He was tough and robust, only about six feet tall, but powerfully sculpted ,with thick cords of muscle running the length of his body. When he looked at a person, they wanted to take a step back from the power blasted at them. Under it all, though, he was a sweet-tempered guy.

Until he turned into a Kodiak bear, obviously.

"Hi Sasha, good to see you." Tim opened his arms for a hug.

His people were huggers and handshakers, which I loved. I hadn't gotten a lot of that growing up, so I took advantage of it. I gave him a big squeeze, having really gotten comfortable with him these last couple months. He always made time for me, pleased that I wanted to get to know his people and personally thank his fighters for keeping me alive when we battled Trek, the white mage, in the woods.

He also understood that sometimes I needed to get away from Stefan's people, who thought humans were mostly worthless. Granted, when you could manipulate and control most of the species, and were simultaneously kept down by them—having to skulk off to the shadows—yeah, I got it. But still, hanging out with other humans, regardless of if they turned into soft creatures with wet noses, kept a girl sane.

He turned to his left and motioned for two others to get up. "This is Jack, the tiger you rode like a horse."

I felt my face flush. "More like a gurney," I mumbled.

Jack stepped forward with balanced grace, something I didn't expect from a stocky, barrel-chested man swinging muscular arms. His gold-hazel eyes connected with mine, giving me a weird kind of thrill—like being stalked on a prairie somewhere. "It was a pleasure fighting beside you."

"Or under you, like a pony," Jonas rumbled from beside the door, staring straight ahead in his "I am ignoring all things human or *Mata*" default pose.

I rolled my eyes. To Jack I said, "Don't mind him, he's just mad no one likes him."

Jonas clenched his jaw.

"And Ann, whom you know, I believe," Tim went on with a smirk.

Ann stepped forward with a beaming smile, her customary shock of blue hair, and a hug. "Hi! Long time no see."

"It's been a week," I laughed.

"Yeah. A week without a girl my own speed to talk to. I just have these grim party poopers."

Tim cleared his throat, eliciting an evil smile from Ann.

"Well, cool," I said, bobbing my head, happy to be alive. I

had friends, a clan, a handsome boyfriend and a guy that wanted to adopt me—my life was turning out a-okay.

To Ann I said, "At least I have someone that gets my sense of humor."

"Everyone else will come around, trust me," she replied.

"Doubtful." Jonas stepped forward, suddenly action. "Let's get going. I got things to do."

"I *am* your things to do," I shot back as Jonas grabbed me by the arm and hauled me toward the door.

"I know. And you're getting behind."

"Our working relationship is not exactly professional," I muttered as Jonas walked me out of the house and left me at the driver's side door of a giant black Hummer.

"What, not going to open the door for me?" I asked sarcastically as I pulled open the door and scrambled up inside. The responding glare shut me up.

We rolled up to a decrepit building in the industrial part of town. The structure stood in the middle of the run-down block, crumbling and abandoned. Jagged windows dotted the face, littering broken glass on the dirty sidewalk lining its front. Boards covered the doors and graffiti marred the pock-marked brick.

We got out of the car and surveyed the building for a moment, waiting for Tim and the others to pull up. "Quaint," I said in a hush, scooting closer to Jonas.

Jonas stalked toward the boarded front door, his feet crunching glass and debris into the hard pavement. The sounds echoed along the quiet street, pinging off the walls and disintegrating into the silence. I followed, knowing that with him around, the only people in their right mind who would pick a fight with us were his kind of people. I could handle magic workers; it was the gun carriers I was concerned about—my kind.

"You okay?" Tim asked, stepping beside me and rubbing my back to calm my nerves.

"No sweat. Kinda. So...why are we here, again? Territory breach?"

Jack and Ann split up, each walking in a diagonal line toward the opposite corners of the building.

"Stefan had reports of a breach, but we have two pack members missing. Last we know, they were in this part of town. We're wondering if the two are related," Tim informed me, his acute focus scanning the building in front of us.

A loud screech echoed down the street as Jonas ripped off the board across the front entryway. His arms and back bunched with thick, lethal muscle. The wood groaned as it bent, hanging on with steel claws. It was no match for Jonas' strength, though. A moment later, the board flew to the side, jarring my teeth as it banged off the concrete and slid to a stop.

I took two loud breaths as silence once again descended on our surroundings. If anyone was around, we'd just made our presence known.

Jack disappeared beyond the corner of the building. A moment later, Ann did, too.

"Sasha—" Jonas motioned me near. He stepped into the gaping black of the doorway.

"Oh *man*," I whined, tiptoeing closer.

Tim stayed at my back, eyes scanning the street and then the darkened face of the building. Jonas spared him one irritated glance before honing in on me.

"I need you to sense for magic. Something doesn't feel right, and it *certainly* doesn't smell right. It's too subtle for me to pick up, though."

"Do I have to go inside?" I whispered. I rubbed my arms as the lifeless building pressed down around me. It felt hollowed, somehow. Gutted and left for dead.

Jonas stared at me for a long, stern-faced beat. "Yes."

I pushed the air out of my lungs, a swear riding the wave. I could sprint into danger with a grin and a rape whistle, but this slow creeping into the unknown was not high on my list of loves.

Goosebumps spread across my arms as I crossed the threshold, a feeling of disquiet smearing over my skin like lotion. I barely heard Jonas' voice speaking to Tim as the cold, dank air washed over me. "Your magic will throw things off, mongrel. Stay outside."

Tim growled out some sort of threat, but I couldn't focus on that now. Prickles dotted my exposed flesh, foul magic eating through my senses. Jonas had it right: something was definitely off.

I put out my hands in front of me like a blind person feeling their way in. The rush of power, slippery and hard to control, filled my body as I called the elements, combating the polluted power in the room with blissful joy. My foot went lopsided on a discarded board, popping it out from under my shoe, skittering across the floor in a dull collection of tinkles.

The shadows crouched in the corners of the enormous, empty space, watching me. Moonlight filtered in from jagged, broken windows along the outside of the structure, casting an unearthly glow. My breath rang through my ears, unnaturally loud, interrupting the stillness of a tomb.

This was a very bad idea. I could feel it. How did I land myself in this job, again?

Filling my lungs and then holding it, I inched closer to the back of the warehouse. Large beams crossed above me and touched down periodically, keeping the sagging ceiling in place far above my head. A ring of black along the side wall advertised an old firepit for someone down on their luck. I kept my eyes pointed down, wary of needles and other items lazily discarded after a night of partying.

As I got halfway through the open space, a vulgar feeling began to crawl up my skin like tiny insects. The sickly sweet smell of rotting flesh tickled my nose.

"I've never felt anything like this before," I said quietly, passing my hands through the air. "Although, granted, I haven't had a lot of experience."

Shapes took form within the shadows toward the back wall the closer I got. On the right, near the corner of the building, lay a pile of grayish sticks, charred and blackened by fire. Scorched fabric was glued to the various elements of the pile.

Three more steps had me halting, sucking in a huge breath.

It was a body! They weren't sticks, they were bones coated in masticated skin!

Did that moan come from me?

A face, twisted in an endless scream of agony, lay on the backside of his calves. One arm had been ripped out of the socket and lay flat under his back. One leg, cracked at the thigh, lay over the other. He was broken and twisted, as if he'd been made of matchsticks and sporadically snapped and tossed to the ground.

"No human could have done this," I whispered. "His back was broken in half."

"A bear could have," Jonas' voice echoed around the crouching walls.

"Not without opposable thumbs," I retorted into the hush.

A few more steps and I could see another fire site, only this time, there was a large black pot overturned against the wall. A round camping stove, smudged with soot, half lay under it.

"This has got to be a few days old, at least..."

"You're not here to investigate," Jonas growled. "You're here to feel for magic. We have an experienced clan that'll go over this site and give us more conclusive findings."

"Oh. Well, you could've made that more clear before I looked at the body."

I let my magic drift, sensing for spells and pitfalls within the area. This was something I practiced every day per Toa's instruction. A large part of my job was sensing other magic and possible dangers. I still had trouble doing this on the fly, but here, in the quiet settings, the building almost feeling as if it was holding its breath, I had nothing else to do but concentrate.

The black glow of my magic, hardly discernable in the gloom of the warehouse, drifted over the overturned pot. Like a match to kerosene, a circular fire lit up, climbing into the sky. Sparkles danced and played in a shimmering orange halo lazily drifting toward the right. Toward the body.

I could not help that squeak. Or holding my breath afterwards.

Still it drifted. Reaching for that death. What would it do when it got there?

I didn't want to know!

A blast of rotten stench crawled up my nose, prompting a gag. That smell didn't come from the body; it came from the disgusting magic corroding this area. Magic that was still active. Lingering, waiting. But for what? Whatever spells had been laid, they weren't used to create rainbows. They were also extensive and intricate. Beyond my training.

"Not good magic over here..." I mumbled.

My magic spread like a fog over the body. For a second, nothing happened.

"Sasha?" Tim asked into the din.

"Don't go in there, mong—"

Jonas' voice cut off as my magic started to sizzle and pop. Like water splashing into hot grease.

"What's it doing?" I asked Jonas with a quiver in my voice.

"This isn't normal..." Jonas' voice drifted away.

"Back out of there, Sasha," Tim urged from the door.

Something tugged at my magical senses. It was like undertow, rolling and fierce, sucking. Consuming. As fast as magic surged into my body, elements desperate to get in, something in that area stole it again, using my draw to fuel itself.

"Crap," I mumbled, scrabbling to pull my power back.

"What is it?" Jonas asked, stepping into the building, his tattoos lighting up like a Christmas tree. A great, gleaming sword swung into his hand, the blade glowing orange.

"Get out of here, Jonas! I need to tie off this weird spell. It's sucking magic to it."

Jonas took a hasty step back, his body once again receding out of the doorway. Tim backed out with him, but hesitantly.

I got to work, sweat beading my brow, fighting the draw both of that corner, and from the elements fighting to rush into my body.

"Nasty spell-working, this," I said under my breath, sensing the elements within the casting. "They're, like, *reaching* for me. Feeding off my magic. I've never dealt with a spell like this. I didn't even know this was possible."

"Dark magic," Jonas whispered. "Hard to work. Harder to control. Someone has balls of steel."

"Well, it's not me," I wheezed.

I snubbed out the elements that made up the spell, like soldering wires, closing the spell in a sort of circuit.

"I don't think the wielder knew exactly what he was doing," I murmured, analyzing the lacy structure of the orangey incantation. It hovered within a shaky line spilled on the cement floor. *Spilled* because it looked suspiciously like blood, sticky and slick, gleaming in the soft light from the window.

As I was about to turn away toward Jonas, wanting to talk about what I'd done, the lacy spell cleared away like mist. In its place grinned the head of a black monster, staring at me like a hungry lion would a fresh steak.

"You did not call me." Sharp, ragged teeth filled a mouth too big for its face.

Terror jolted me back as a stringy leg stepped forward.

"Sasha?" Jonas' voice held hard fibers of alarm as it echoed through the cavernous space.

The monster slapped into an invisible barrier. Orange sparks rained down on its head as a tall circle flared to life around it. It glanced up, and then around, noticing the hazy orange circle trapping it. And then its face straightened out, staring right at me out of black pits instead of eyes. In a raspy voice that shivered across my body, it said, "We can rule, you and I. Our power, combined, will be indestructible. Join me."

"Oh lovely, one of you. Fantastic."

I eyed its cage as it did, sensing the weakness of it. The shaky spell barely held together. Even as I stood there, the thing was starting to eat away at its cage.

Super.

Was this a terrible spell by design, or some sort of failed attempt?

"We gotta get out of here!" I roared at Jonas, backing away as quickly as possible. "This thing is way, *way* stronger than other *Dulcha* I've seen. It's feeding off of the magic containing it, somehow. We need Toa for this one."

Jonas flicked his gaze at Tim, whose eyes were directed in a flat stare, at the scary monster pacing within its sphere. "You wanna go check if the dead body is one of yours?"

Tim started forward immediately. When that thing's hollow gaze locked on him, his step did not falter.

"Don't touch the orange cylinder surrounding it," I whisper-yelled as he passed.

"When he's done, pull your magic out, but you'll need to seal off the building," Jonas instructed as I neared.

"Yes, Jonas, I know. I'm not an idiot."

His face had turned to point down at me, the area around his eyes tight.

"This isn't just a normal *Dulcha,* is it?" I asked in a tiny voice, following Jonas as he backed away from the opening. My eyes scanned the enormity of the building. I thought of the spells at my disposal—the ones I could do well. "I'm not really sure how to seal off something of this size. I mean, containment spell, obviously, but it seems to be eating away at the one locking it in right now. How did the wielder create that thing?"

"Old magic," Jonas said in a low voice, stepping aside so a grim-faced Tim could exit the door and move past. "More power makes the process easier, but humans that don't know how to work their magic can call them, too. It takes chants and sacrifices. Blood and death."

His haunted eyes took me in. "I'm only orange. You are black. If that thing breaks free, my magic isn't going to stop it. Which means you need to work this shit out. That thing cannot escape this building."

I grimaced. True words.

"Don't blow up the building, either," he added. "It'll laugh at the fire and keep on coming."

I groaned. "That didn't need to be said..."

We backed out to the center of the quiet street, the shape changers all waiting for us.

Tim's gaze touched mine, tight and serious, before finding Jack. "It was Dom in there. He didn't make it to his fox form. He was a fast and fearless fighter. No chains or manacles to secure him."

"How did he get taken so easily? Do your people get manipulated like humans do?" I asked, because that would be a good explanation.

Tim shook his head solemnly.

"I found Phillip," Ann said quietly. "Killed with a sword. Apparently he was just in the way."

"The person that called this thing didn't need two sacrifices—one was enough," Jonas growled, gaze skewering the decrepit and hulking warehouse in front of us. "Seal this place off, Sasha."

Him using my name straightened my back and sent tingles down my spine. His eyes, a dark shade of brown with specks of gold, were intense and serious, a spark of fear deep within their depths. That thing in the warehouse had shaken him. Shaken Jonas, the meanest, most fearsome badass in Stefan's clan.

Not good.

Survival mode washed over me, that glimmer of fear peeking out of Jonas' stare infusing my courage. I had to stop that thing from getting out. Only seriously bad news could scare Jonas, and only I had the ability to cut it off.

It was not shaping into a good day.

I opened up and let the elements rush in, filling me to capacity, then taking just a bit more. For me, unlike for others, magic shock was a very real issue every single time I used my magic. I couldn't draw too heavily, or the dam would burst, the elements blasting into my body until my body became overloaded and shut down. So far, that shut down was just for a few hours, or even a day or so. I'd been lucky. Worst case, however, meant that the shutdown would be forever. I had to be careful.

I envisioned placing a huge blanket over that warehouse, draping it in suffocating power. No holes. The weave was water tight. I used mass quantities of earth for the lock, keeping that spell put.

I'd learned a thing or two from Toa. It had given me stress wrinkles, but I was getting somewhere.

As the billowing cloud of magic enveloped the building, I could feel my energy sucking out of my body. I had limitless magic, yes, but like running or lifting something heavy, it took energy. I did not have limitless energy. It was another way things could go wrong.

For all the things I had going for me in the magic world, I had just as many that would result in death if I wasn't careful. I was forever walking on that razor's edge.

I reached through my link with Stefan, tugging, needing his special power. The distance softened the connection, lessening his help, but he was with me immediately, balancing the flow. Distributing it.

He was also growing concerned. This was supposed to be a routine stop along his—our—territory. I shouldn't need his help. That I did would alert him something was wrong.

Gaining a burst of energy, I sprinkled an invisibility charm that would have the eye glancing off of the building should someone wander by. I also tied off this spell, keeping the magic in place. I stepped back, panting with fatigue.

Jonas' brow had furrowed. "You did more than just disguise it, right?"

I continued my eye-rolling marathon as Tim stalked up, having left with Ann around the building when I started my spell. "Obviously."

"There's nothing obvious when you do magic..."

"He was taken down cleanly," Tim said, glancing around the area.

"What were they doing here?" Jonas asked suspiciously.

"We had notice of a wilder in this location. They came to check it out."

Jonas and Tim stared at each other for a moment, before Jonas took one more glance at the building and headed back to the car. "C'mon, we gotta let the Boss know."

A thrill ran through my stomach at the mention of Stefan. As always, I couldn't wait to get back to him. It was like an extended honeymoon period with him—part of me wanted to just hang out in the same room and stare at him while drool dribbled down my chin.

At the moment, however, unease ate away my longing to touch him. He knew something was wrong, and he wanted me away from whatever it was. Like any alpha male, he was protective and possessive to a fault, wanting to wrap me up in bubble wrap and stow me away from harm. Obviously that was as harebrained as it was impossible, but it didn't prevent his agitation when he couldn't protect me.

Scared Jonas on one hand, partially irrational clan leader struggling for control on the other. The day was not getting any better.

As I turned toward the car, Tim said, "We'll hang on—I want to see to Phillip's remains."

Jonas nodded and motioned for me to hurry up and get in the car.

"Alright, this is your time to assert yourself," Jonas coached as he started driving. "This is an important and valid discovery that you made."

"We did it together—"

"*You* are the Black Mage, which means you technically led this expedition. You are in charge—"

"Which no one can tell since you constantly bully me."

"—and you need to demonstrate that if the Boss has people around him. You need to start showing that you pull rank with everyone but the Boss. Got it?"

"Yes."

"You need to act mature and professional. Can you do that?"

Not a chance. "Absolutely."

We pulled up to the front of the mansion, only a faint glow seeping from the front windows. Jonas slammed the gear shift into park and opened the door. "Alright, let's go."

Ten minutes later, we arrived at the room my link told me Stefan occupied. Jonas stepped forward and pulled open the door. I got an impatient thumb jerk from him, telling me to enter. As I crossed the threshold; the world fell away. All I could focus on were those intelligent, dark eyes, looking at me out of that earth-shatteringly handsome face. My stomach exploded in butterflies as my chest tugged, wanting to close the distance and touch him. The emotion through the link held the same longing, the same single-minded focus as Stefan paid homage to me entering the room.

In the beginning, this would irritate people to no end, no one understanding why everything ground to a halt so we could share a moment meeting our other half. After Stefan scared the crap out of a few people for interrupting, or I accidentally zapped them with magic, they all got the hint. It only lasted about thirty seconds, but in that time, nothing existed in the world but each other.

"*And* they're back," Charles said as I exhaled, taking in the scene.

Stefan stood near the far wall, holding a sheet of paper with that sexy muscular arm. His rippled body stood in repose, in the middle of some business meeting that must have to do with our journey in a few weeks, because all of the top army guys and gals, including my new adopted dad and his staring side-kick, were present. Stefan's slacks fit him oh-so-right, showing off that defined butt and his strong thighs. A dress shirt strained across his enormous width of shoulders and hinted at his mouthwatering pecs. Those washboard abs were hidden, but I salivated knowing they were there.

"Having a hot flash?" Charles asked with a smirk, the only one allowed to back talk to me in Stefan's presence.

Charles had been through serious crap on my behalf—he'd earned it.

"Sorry, where were we?" I swung my gaze around the crowded room.

"We were discussing the needs of the clan in our absence," Stefan said smoothly, eyes devouring me instead of going back to his paper.

I cleared my throat and noticed an intense stare from Jonas. *Oh yeah. Lead.*

"Well, we might need to put that on hold. We found something." I just barely left off the uncertain, "is that okay?"

Stefan's eyes cleared of heat. Anxiety crept back into the link, having disappeared when I arrived in one piece. "What is it?"

I quickly ran through what we found at the warehouse, watching carefully as Stefan's face got grimmer and grimmer with some emotion he was trying desperately to suppress. The link warred with shock and fear and determination. When I finished, more than a few people, including Dominicous, were subtly glancing at him.

"You contained it?" Stefan asked in a low voice.

I nodded. "But we need to get rid of it somehow."

Determination took over the link as his jaw set. "You stay here. I'll deal with it."

"She has to remove her charm," Jonas said in as small of a voice as I'd ever heard him use.

Stefan's gaze skewered Jonas.

"Orange was containing it," I rushed in quickly, knowing

Stefan didn't want me anywhere near that monster, and also knowing the decision came from a man in love, not a leader. Nothing would undermine me faster than if Stefan tried to put Baby in the corner.

"If it escaped orange power, then Jonas wouldn't be any good, since he is also orange. It's my job, Stefan." I straightened my back against that scorching, dominating stare. My warning butt tingle sounded, screaming at me to *flee*. Still I stood my ground, nearly letting terrified chuckles escape my throat to let the tension out of my body.

That intense, black-eyed gaze retracted before he grudgingly nodded. I took a silent breath, trying to ignore the sweat dripping down my back.

"Let's go." Stefan moved across the room. "Jonas, assemble a team. Charles—"

Stefan cut off, his eyes flicking to me. Jonas was staring again.

Oh yeah. Lead.

"Charles, get Adnan," I jumpstarted. "You two are mine so Stefan can use Jonas."

Stefan gave me the briefest of nods, indicating I did the right thing. Thank god.

"You're going to take a juvenile for protection?" Claudia, a red power with a mean right hook, came as close to a snicker as was possible for it not to be a challenge.

I stared her down, trying to get my gaze to shock into her like Stefan's always did. Condescension stared back.

"You'll challenge him to a duel tomorrow," I noted smoothly. "We'll see how you hold up against a juvenile. I will personally tell you you're right if you win. Now," my gaze swept the room, "let's get going. That thing was too smug for my taste."

CHAPTER TWO

"What did Jonas have to say?" Toa asked in his silky tone as he drifted in beside Dominicous.

Dominicous slowed his pace, allowing Stefan and Sasha to lead their fierce-eyed warriors out of the mansion. If he kept to the front, his position would dictate his leadership. Stefan was barely keeping his subservience in check as it was; if Dominicous took control of a situation as dire as this, the younger male would challenge for sure. And while usually that wouldn't be a huge deal—Dominicous able to quell most upstarts easily—he wasn't entirely positive he would come out the victor. Even if he did, however, he didn't want to leave his adopted daughter without her future mate. A challenge needed to be prevented at all costs.

"This is probably a class-six demon. Weak enough, but based on what Sasha said, operating with some strange magic." Toa glided out the front door with a smooth and calm demeanor. Most wouldn't notice the left shoulder raised slightly above the right, a sign of Toa's tense and unsure state of mind.

Very little ruffled Toa.

"That isn't an altogether strong demon," Dominicous said calmly. "With it contained for now, and with Stefan's ability to organize and lead in battle, we shouldn't have any problem dispatching it."

"*We* shouldn't, no." Toa's gaze drifted toward Sasha, walking with a sure step toward one of the many parked cars.

Dominicous knew she had no idea what she was walking toward, but she kept her chin up and back straight. *Such a courageous young woman.*

"The demon will hone in on her, I am certain," Toa continued. "Usually, only someone that summoned the demon can converse with it."

"Speaking with it means one can control it, correct? Why isn't this beneficial?"

Toa made a disgusted sound at Dominicous' ignorance. "It could be beneficial, yes. It could. But it is a two-way affair. You can speak, but you can also understand. And if you aren't strong enough to control, you will become the controlled. Sasha has barely emerged into our way of life, into leadership, into her magic—and now we are throwing demons at her. She barely has time to grasp one idea when we throw something else at her. How can we expect her to keep up?"

Toa smoothed his hair, and Dominicous knew he was trying to smooth his nerves at the same time. Toa had to be out in front of her training-wise to give all of them any hope of her making it through the council meeting in one piece, but so many other dangers kept arising. Toa was a perfectionist, and often contemplative, but he'd been having to sprint to the next challenge right along with Sasha. He didn't have to tell Dominicous that it was getting to him—Dominicous could feel it all through their blood link. But they each had their duties, and all duties had a hard road as far as Sasha was concerned.

"You fear Sasha can be thus turned?" Dominicous asked quietly, trying to keep them on track.

Toa's mouth collapsed into a thin, bloodless line. "I am not sure. She has not dealt with a demon of this magnitude. *Dulcha* do not even remotely compare."

Dominicous shook his head as a chorus of car doors shut around him. "She will not turn. She has a core of steel to her."

"Then it will attempt to destroy her. Without someone to control it, it is a free entity, able to rip, rape, and pillage as it will. She will be target number one."

"This isn't the age of Vikings, Toa." Dominicous suppressed a chuckle, starting the car and pulling away from the curb. His partner at arms had always been a little...overdramatic when edging up to a battle. It was a side of him not many saw. "Plus, it won't come anywhere near her. Stefan will see to that long before I would have to intervene and ensure it."

"Dominicous—" Toa's nostrils flared. "You take things too lightly. It will target her. Her defensive...talents will spring to life. She will try to dispatch it on her own, feeling out the spell like a blind man searches for a telephone. Like she has with *Dulcha*. It will sap her energy and rip the life out of her before she can complete the spell."

Dominicous cleared his throat. "She has Stefan to fortify her magic until we can link. She will have plenty of power for a five or six-level demon. Toa, I really think—"

"I cannot link with her."

Dominicous' head whipped around. The car swerved to the right before Dominicous ripped the wheel back. "In all this time, you, a white, have not enacted the age-old partnership between a black and a white? You realize, I am sure, that the more one person links with another, the easier and more effective the bond. At the council there will be a great many trying to link with her to create just such a bond. You have the privilege of having her all to yourself, and you *have not linked?"*

Toa's stare drifted across the space of the car and held his, unwaveringly. Dominicous pulled to the side, idling. The car crackled with magic, the challenge in Toa's eyes making the hair stand up all over Dominicous' body.

"We've been here before, Toa," Dominicous said in a low tone. "I will take this moment to remind you that, despite your higher level of power, you do not usually come out on top in these instances."

Toa's gaze retracted slightly, but he did not drop it altogether. Nor did he speak. Dominicous had offended him. Damn.

"I was bold in my allegations." It was as close as Dominicous would come to an apology.

That icy blue stare held. And held.

Finally, the blond head bowed ever so slightly. He turned back to the road. Dominicous pushed the gas pedal.

Into the purr of the large motor, Toa said, "Pairing with a black should be effortless. It was how we were made, after all. And I can see how this could be a possibility, but she is a magic conductor. She is wired differently. When I link, I give that raging torrent of magic another outlet. I give it more body to fill. It gushes through her and directly into me. It's... chaos. There is no controlling it—I do not know how she manages. I have tried three times, and all three times ended up flat on my back. She, *she,* had to cut it off and rip it away. The novice had to protect the master."

"And this torrent—this is something she deals with on a daily basis?"

"Yes. Like trying to direct a flood. It is the price for the power at her disposal, I am sure. With her as lead, we could have a huge Merge. She doesn't have to pull the power and disperse it, or merge with anyone to pull more, she simply has to open up, and direct the deluge."

Dominicous shook his head. "Is this because she is human? Because she is black?"

"No. It is because she is one in a million. Had we known what we found that night, the little thing you gave blood to, we would've taken her right then. We would've had time to train her, to study her. To coach her before she could come up with wild ways to use her power."

"That day is done. We are here now. What do we do? Link around her?"

"And then there is Stefan to think about."

Dominicous threw the car in park beside Sasha's vehicle. He breathed through his mouth in a silent exhale, willing patience in the light of Toa's constant analytics. Stefan stepped out of a large Hummer on their right, his face a mask of fierce determination. Dominicous could almost see the ghosts of his parents sitting on his shoulders as his gaze stabbed Charles, the driver of Sasha's vehicle.

Toa said, "He can balance Sasha. Her special skill seems to be to coax others to accept more magic. His special skill is to balance the flow of magic. He gets more power while balancing her so she can work the torrents accosting her. They make each other better—more powerful. They were made for each other. One in a million."

Dominicous snorted at the romantic babble. He earned a glare.

"If he had been a white..." Toa's voice drifted away as he watched Stefan consult with Jonas. Charles sat in the car, speaking with Sasha. Probably filling her in on what she faced.

"Stefan is not in control," Dominicous stated flatly. "He was not there when his parents died, but he lost everything.

Imagination is sometimes worse than witnessing the actual events."

Toa threaded his fingers together in his lap. "It might be wise, for all our sakes, if you lead this battle."

"He would challenge me, immediately. He would see the value in my leadership, but he would fear for Sasha's safety if he wasn't in control."

"But he's not in control."

"He's holding it together."

"She will try to cut that thing off from the source before I can enact a link with you. I will then have to try and work around her magical weave without merging. Dominicous, if you sit and do nothing, it could kill her, and then everyone else. If I scrape against her magic, it will bind to me and surge through me. I'll end up flat on my back, but this time, without the novice to save me. You'll then be fighting without me."

"So we chop the thing into bits while you two play at elements. It's not that strong of a demon, Toa. You're fantasizing."

Toa exhaled noisily. The glare was back. "Can you take nothing seriously? I wonder how you were able to ascend to your position at all."

"You know how: by killing. C'mon, I want to be in position to monitor my daughter. I've just found her again, I will not lose her."

CHAPTER THREE

Charles sat in the car after the Boss evacuated, feeling uncertainty and nerves burning a hole in his stomach. Sasha sat beside him, picking her nail and watching the Boss as he gathered his men to him.

Charles had just explained what it was they faced, but the problem was, he didn't really know, either. He'd learned about this stuff in school. That, and from the rumors and the hushed stories told in places the Boss was sure never to hear. This wasn't one of those things people wanted to get caught talking about.

"So..." Her voice was frail, sounding as nervous as Charles felt. "It's kind of like a *Dulcha*, then. This thing. Right?"

"This thing is not like a *Dulcha*," Charles answered. "Well, it is, but in a different sort of way. A *Dulcha* is a newer creation with magic—implanting a demon into a human body. Demons that need a host—need to feed off of a life—are lesser demons. No real power. No real ability to think on their own. They're governed by the magic holder that summoned them."

"Trek always did that."

"Exactly. And they reacted to his desires. As demons get more powerful, they need a sacrifice, but not a host. These demons are also less likely to take directions. They're harder to control. Plus, it's the old magic. Think of it like opening a portal to that underworld you believe in. Let one of these magical beings with a lot of power run around, and it'll rain down death and destruction."

"Why? What's their purpose? What do they want?"

Charles squinted at her. "Ah...good question. I never thought to ask."

Adnan shifted in the back seat. Charles glanced at him in the rear view mirror and got a blank expression in return. He obviously didn't know, either.

Sasha said, "Okay, well, how do I get rid of it? Toa hasn't taught me how to link, yet."

Charles stared at her. "He hasn't?"

Sasha chewed her lip in response.

Oh. Toa probably tried, but something went wrong. Figured. With her, something always went all kinds of wrong before it finally went right.

He said as much.

"Really helpful, Charles, great talk."

"At least you have a little information. If it was up to the Boss, you'd be back at home base."

Sasha turned to him in a cloud of frustration. "What is really going on, Charles? Why is he so freaked—"

Her mouth slammed shut and her body went rigid. Her eyes flicked toward her left—Adnan. She could be open with Charles—they were as close as siblings—but Adnan was a different story entirely. And he must've known it.

"See you out there," he said quickly. He slid out of the car and closed the door behind him, waiting just outside.

"What is his deal with all this?" she asked immediately,

fear riding her words. "Why is he scared out of his head, Charles? What's happening?"

"He's, ah..."

Charles hesitated. This was the Boss' business, and that man hadn't opened his mouth to utter a word about it since it happened. Apparently not even to his lady love, which meant he didn't want the information known. Charles was not about to get killed by being the messenger.

Although, not telling her anything and letting her get her fool self killed would also get him, as her protector, killed.

How did he always end up in these situations?

"You know his parents were killed, right?" Charles hedged.

Sasha's round eyes swung his way. Charles nodded. "Without giving too much detail—or any, because I value my life—I'll just say that his parents had a run-in with one of these things, and it didn't work favorably on his family life. You need to approach with caution on this one, Sasha."

"Oh my god—demons killed his parents?"

Charles wiggled like fire ants were eating his backside. "I've said plenty."

"A demon like the one in there? Is it that strong—or, you know, that powerful?"

"Jonas said that this one is probably a six or seven, out of ten. *Dulcha* are nines and tens—not powerful. This one is just slightly more so. The one that...you know...with his parents—gods, I shouldn't be telling you this."

"I won't breathe a word."

"I'm sure he can feel your gushy compassion and all that chick crap."

"Oh, shut up." She punched him. "You feel those things, too, you jackass."

Charles rubbed his arm for something to do. Mental note: teach her how to punch. "Anyway, the demon that..."

"I get it. Finish the damn sentence."

"Well, it was a three, I think. A really nasty one. They had to sacrifice three people to *summon* it—two humans called it, the lunatics. Guess who it killed first? Served them right."

"So the one we have isn't that strong. But, are you sure? Because Jonas was really freaked out. And Stefan is out of his mind…"

"Jonas lost his dad," Charles said without thinking. He thrust a finger through the silent air, straight into her face. "If you say one word—*one word*—to anyone that I just told you that, I will make your life hell. Do you understand me?"

"No you won't, because Jonas would've already killed you."

True. Shit.

Worry melted the grin off her face. She peered at the large building a ways in front of him, then at the Boss. "What are we waiting for?"

As if on cue, the Boss' gaze flashed into the car and pommeled Charles. Charles could feel the power push into his body, buckling his spine and having his gaze headed for the ground before he could stop himself. This was the Boss that everyone feared. Everyone. The mean sonovabitch that fought his way to the leadership role with teeth and nails, taking down males twice his age, experience, and size. If he found someone he couldn't cripple with brute force, he used his honed intellect. That failing, he used his friends.

Jonas and Jameson had been infallible wingmen, Charles had heard. Still were.

The Boss had started ascending shortly after his parents were killed. He wanted to make sure no other kid would go through what he did. And so far, he had.

But he hadn't had a demon show up to prove his prowess. Until now. With his chick on site. And not only that, but she'd have to actually face the demon, too.

Charles should have picked another occupation.

Knowing what was coming, Charles spilled out of the car as he clicked on the child lock, slamming the locked door before Sasha could follow. The large, lethal shape of his leader came around the hood, bristling with danger. He did not look scared at all. He looked formidable.

Charles gulped.

"If shit goes sideways, get her out of here," the Boss growled, putting a heavy hand on the door in an act of protectiveness, keeping Sasha from letting herself out. "I don't care if you have to knock her out and run, *get her out*."

"No problem, Boss."

Charles felt the dark stare as the Boss ensured those words were heard. When he tore his gaze away to walk to the front line, Charles couldn't help a sigh of relief. Only to be sucked back up when the crazy sidekick stalked up next.

"You keep her alive, or you better hope you go down with her," Jonas threatened, his eyes alight with his thirst for blood.

"Don't tell me my job, bro. I got this." Charles flexed, wishing that other male's stare didn't have the power to give him the heebie-jeebies. Jonas could really turn into a hardass when he placed himself as a protector of someone. Especially someone in danger. Like the pissed off human in the car.

The scar on Jonas' neck stood out in relief as he smirked. He didn't spare a glance for the hard rapping on the inside of the window.

Charles took a deep breath after both males had moved on. "Well, goody, rainbows and unicorns. Lovely working conditions."

He opened the door to a bag of cats.

"What the hell, Charles?!" Sasha yelled, clambering out. "I'm supposed to be his damn equal, and the two of you lock me in the car?"

"Sorry, he's bigger. C'mon." Feigning confidence, Charles

jerked his head toward the warehouse. "Dominicous is already out of his car and headed over there. You need to show up before he does."

"Why, would he usurp my power or something?"

"Yes. Him hanging back is a nod to the Boss. And you. He is letting everyone know that the Boss is leading—why do you not know this?"

"I can't learn everything in a few months, Charles. Magic came first. Stupid hierarchy of egotistical penises had to take a backseat."

"Penises don't have egos. And what about the women in command? They can be pretty damn bitchy."

"The women have bigger balls than you do, Charles. Let's get focused."

Kind of a dick thing to say.

The warehouse crouched on the deserted road, silent and foreboding, housing some sort of hellion that could tear families apart. He had never seen one, true, but from a lifetime of ghost stories, he wasn't in a great hurry. He liked the little life he'd set up—he didn't really want it getting torn apart right now.

They stepped beyond the cars. A large circle of *Mata* waited around the warehouse, facing the building. They stood sentinel with resolute expressions and fisted hands, just in case that thing inside got out. Dressed in loose sweats, with most primed to change form, they waited for war.

Walking toward each *Mata* guard, ready to take over, was a clan member dressed in battle leathers with glowing swords.

The *Mata* didn't plan to step aside. The clan members would try to make them.

"What a mess," Sasha muttered.

Charles agreed wholeheartedly. "I thought you used a concealment charm?"

Adnan caught up with them, shadowing Sasha.

"I took it off when we got here. Remember me yelling at you to shut it so I could concentrate?" Sasha rubbed her temples, her nerves fraying, looking every bit as out of her element as Charles felt.

In front of the building, facing off, stood the Boss and Tim. The Boss was bigger, more heavily muscled, with an elegance to his grace that made a male's hairs stand on end—he was a world ender.

But Tim...Charles had to hand it to him. He wasn't a wimp by anyone's standards, especially when he changed into that colossal Kodiak bear. He faced off, meeting the Boss' stare with one of his own, power and brawn ready to be unleashed.

"C'mon," Sasha said, half to herself. She marched out toward the two men.

"What's going on?" she demanded as she got within speaking range.

It was Tim that answered. "Stefan has decided he reins this territory, and as such, is trying to send us packing. I have politely informed him, as is my place, that when we lose one of ours, we are given license to step in. This was an agreement reached in witness of Dominicous and his authority of office as it represents the council."

Sasha stepped forward to make a point. The Boss held out his hand to block her advance, trying to keep her at a safer distance.

"*Back off!*" She pushed at the Boss' arm. Her brows lowered dangerously when she had no effect. Next they heard a metallic crackle, *zapping* the Boss with a shot of fire as only she knew how.

The big male took one step back, every muscle on his body taut in pain. Jonas, standing a few feet away, rolled his neck—he'd flown three feet when Sasha had done that to him.

Her gaze slid to Tim as her brows lowered. "You, too."

Tim stared back for a moment, before taking one step back.

Wise, Charles thought.

"This is *my* rule," she addressed both males. "Tim, you came here as my guest, which makes you subject to my leadership. Had you investigated on your own, per the signed treaties, given that it was only your men affected, then yes, you would be licensed to step in. For right now, until I abandon my rights, you do not take a primary role. Not until the threat is neutralized."

Charles couldn't help his mouth dropping open as Tim nodded, somehow not looking as shocked as Charles felt. Who *was* this girl? And more importantly, who'd been working with her? Genius, whoever it was. And obviously extremely patient.

Her gaze swung to the Boss. "I will repeat, this is *my* rule. I will soon defer to your leadership, since you have more experience in these matters, but regarding the *Mata's* right to be here, I have the rights to approve that, and I do. We do not have time for a challenge, so I hope you don't make one. I woke up whatever that thing is. Somehow. It's loose in that warehouse. I can feel it eating away at my magic. It's doing a really good job."

"The last time these *mongrels* offered aid," the Boss said in low, hate-filled tones, "they whimpered like curs and ran, leaving *us* to deal with it. There is no way I'm leaving holes in the defense. This is easily settled with them leaving now before the demon is released."

The breath left Sasha's body, a brief flash of compassion covering her face. Just as quickly, it was gone; business.

"The pack before me consisted of a loose band of scared individuals," Tim argued. "Our kind don't do well in that setting. I stepped up, disbanded the old regime, and instilled the new order. We aren't cowards, and we do not back down. He's working with haunted memories, no matter how potent. Like a child."

The Boss flexed, probably hating that comment. His gaze flicked toward the warehouse, deciding. Probably realizing it was a hopeless argument with Sasha in control. Finally, he glanced at Sasha without a word.

Picking up the cue immediately, her gaze shifted to the warehouse. "We're out of time."

A strange black mist billowed within the building, creeping out of the broken windows. If not for a glossy sheen containing it, that stuff would've been spilling out onto the street. In the middle of the door, standing on two clawed feet, with long, stringy arms ending in another set of claws, stood a ghastly creature that could only be a demon. It was just as vile and terror-inspiring as Charles had always heard.

It stared at Sasha.

"That black mist is not my magic," Sasha whispered, squinting at the warehouse. "I don't know what it is, but it's not me."

Strange sounds erupted from the gnarled and twisted thing, deep and scratchy. The Boss stepped right to Sasha's side, scary as all hell, ready to protect her with his life. Charles stepped up, too, ready to be her backup line of defense, or her first line of defense—whatever she needed.

"Yeah, right," Sasha answered the thing. Charles felt his magic stir. She was calling the elements. "Plentiful rewards, right? You creeps are all the same. Although, I gotta admit, you are way scarier than the other ones."

Charles felt a cold hand on his shoulder. A pale arm and a flat, blue stare was attached. "We must link. She cannot work the demon on her own," Toa said, an urgency in his gaze Charles had never seen before.

Charles' balls started to tingle in warning. Toa freaked out couldn't be good...

"Is she talking to it?" someone asked in a terrified whisper.

"Who else?" Dominicous asked Toa, his face a stern mask of determination, not unlike the Boss.

"I thought she didn't know how to link?" Charles asked hurriedly, aiming for a steady tone. He didn't really know how, either. He'd only done it in class a million years ago, and that had been under calm conditions, with him already pegged as the clown in class—he didn't have to be serious. This was... different. Unstable. Lives depended on it this time.

"Maybe I should just use my sword," Charles murmured as Sasha took a step toward the thing in the doorway, still staring at her. Still talking to her.

"Hurry!" Toa pushed.

The Boss grabbed Sasha's arm, pulling her into his body. His sword swung out, white with a gold frost, the effect of taking her blood. Within their line, glowing swords came up in a rush, the Boss' readiness an unspoken command. Orange, red, and one green flashed; this crew was packing some power.

Toa shook Charles, knocking him out of uncertainty. "Link, damn you! We are out of time. She is already feeling out the magic attached to the demon!"

He felt a tickle of magical touch as Toa's hand on his bare arm heated up. "I am ready to engage the link. You must reach out to accept it—keep the pool of magic central."

What the hell does that mean?

Charles took a deep breath and pulled a balanced mix of elements. He felt the energy reaching for him, jagged and sticky. Like threading fingers, Charles linked his magic with Toa—surprisingly easier than he expected. Energy swirled between the two of them, yanking at Charles, then pushing.

"Keep it central," Toa said again, his brow furrowed in concentration.

Charles clenched his teeth and wrestled with the flow of elements, trying to move his pool of magic away from his body and along the invisible line of the link between him and Toa, like shoving it out along a tightrope. Their combined effort steadied, shaky but manageable.

"Phew, that wasn't so bad," Charles reflected, too soon.

"Dominicous," Toa said in a monotone.

A blast of power surged through the link from Dominicous, shoving way too much magic Charles' way. He wrestled again, trying to keep it from infusing him and shell-shocking his body. It tried to force its way in, though, tingling along his skin like hot needles, singeing and burning. Too much—it was too much magic!

"Centralize it, you fool!" Toa yelled, his hands balled in fists, sweat standing out on his face.

Charles squeezed his eyes shut and concentrated with everything he had, trying to force it back out along that tight rope. Trying to breathe through the crushing weight of all that magic; trying to rip off his skin and flash-burn his bones.

Inch by inch it went, back to the middle. Balanced, as much as it could be, seemingly hanging out in the air, waiting for Toa to dip in and use it. So much power. So hard to deal with.

Charles longingly grabbed the handle of his sword as Dominicous asked, "Who else?"

"More?" Charles couldn't help the whine. This was way out of his league.

"We only need three of high level," Toa said calmly, once again staring at Sasha. "She is already analyzing the magic."

"Let Toa handle the chants, Sasha," Dominicous commanded in a firm tone.

She didn't acknowledge. Her gaze was locked on that demon, body bowed slightly, brow furrowed.

The demon stared back, its too-large mouth filled with gnarly teeth, grinning manically, always talking. Rasping out incoherent words as she stared.

"Yuck, you're gross. Lots more power than the other ones. But..." Sasha took a few unconscious steps in its direction, as if working out a tough math problem. "You're a runt, aren't you? You aren't all the way here, or something. You're...practice."

"Stop her!" Toa shouted as the Boss pulled her back. She didn't notice any of it.

Which was not like her.

Magic swelled, dragging Charles attention away from Sasha, the power wobbling within the link between the three of them, the bubble of power starting prickles up Charles's arms.

"Focus on the link, Toa, Charles is inexperienced. He is drawing the power to him in his protectiveness." Dominicous stepped forward, up beside Sasha and the Boss, facing the demon. "We don't need him passing out before he can be of use."

The link trembled, the center of magic yanking toward Dominicous. Toa's forehead beaded in sweat.

"Let it loose, Sasha. Let me handle it," Toa instructed.

The thing had started making those horrible sounds again. Like a blade scraping across decaying bones. Black mist spread out along Sasha's magic. Pulsing. A smell of burning hair drifted from the warehouse.

"Oh yeah, I'd get to lead until you got free," Sasha spoke to the demon. "Lot of good vast riches and mind-blowing power gets me, since you'd just suck my power dry and kill a bunch of people. Nah, I think I'll just kill you."

Power surged in Charles, Sasha unconsciously bolstering

him as she always had in classes. They didn't have a link, but they had a deep connection through friendship—she always had him in her unconscious bubble. Except, this time, he wasn't excited about the extra magic.

The link wavered, the extra push from Charles battering toward Toa.

"I cannot maintain this balance with the two of you drawing inconsistently," Toa yelled.

Tim stepped closer to Sasha as he pulled off his sweats, ready to change. Knowing it was coming soon. Whatever happened in the past, Tim was not one to run away, and he was proving it.

"It could be sucking the magic out of her right now," Toa warned. "It uses speech to enact a kind of trance."

"It's not," the Boss growled, still holding her. "She's not expending any energy right now."

The thing started its grating again. Sasha waved her hand through the air. "Right, well, banishing you out of your mobile form might as well be killing you. And guess what, ugly, you aren't real mysterious. Your creator was practicing—I can see that now. You're an experiment gone wrong. You're no stronger than a messenger, isn't that right? All I have to do is..."

"No!" Toa shouted.

The sheen around the building cleared away in an instant, that black plume of smoky vapor spilling out onto the street. Charles could feel it, sucking at him, draining his energy and power even before it touched his skin.

It tumbled forward as the creature surged, rushing, aiming directly for her.

The Boss tossed her behind him, bracing in front of her. Dominicous stood right beside him, sword out, knees bent. A quick blur and blast of magic, and suddenly a Kodiak bear lumbered in the place of Tim. A huge roar rumbled the ground. Bursts of magic lit around the circle, various animals taking the place of their human counterparts. Growls, shrieks and barks sounded a battle roar.

"Cut it down!" the Boss roared.

Glowing swords swung out, three males running forward to cut off the charge. And not a moment too soon.

The maniacally grinning demon reached the first line of defense as the ranks closed in behind it, locking it in a circle of glowing tattoos, swords and fur. A claw struck out with a blur of movement, swiping the midsection of a male with green power. Three gapes in leather bubbled forth a sludge of red, the claws cutting through leather and skin like fingers through foam. Another demon claw swung out, catching a furred arm. The demon snarled, legs whipping out, catching someone on the thigh as a red blade swooped down into the melee.

Magic and metal cut through a thick demon hide, a sizzling swirl of smoke rising from the wound. The howl battered through the street, hate and rage filled. Claws lashed out, downing one male and one wolf.

"No!" Sasha yelled, dagger yanked from its holster. The blade was burnished gold, dimming fast.

"Do not lay that spell, Sasha!" Toa commanded with strain in his voice, his face pale, his hands fisted. His legs wobbled where he stood, trying to balance magic and work it at the same time.

Charles stepped forward, but staggered in a wave of dizziness. Magic pulsed and pushed, yanking at him one minute and pushing the next, threatening to overcome him. Threatening to blast him with more than three times what he could safely handle.

"Include the Boss in this link—he can balance this," Charles said through clenched teeth.

"Hurry, Toa," Dominicous said, knuckles white around the hilt of his sword.

"She is working—something," Toa replied with strain lancing his words. "She is laying intricacies she doesn't understand. She is in survival mode."

A male went down, rolling away. Three steps had the demon halving the distance to Sasha, faster than thought. Claws swinging.

Shit.

Charles staggered forward, skin on fire. Magic scored him like razor blades. Sweat drenched his face.

So this is what the warning stages of magic shock felt like. Now he knew why Sasha wanted to hold back more often than not.

"Almost..." Toa went down on one knee, yanking the magic away from Charles. Trying to keep it centered. Trying to split his focus. To play Superman.

Dominicous stepped forward with Stefan, shaky on his feet, ready to combat the demon regardless of the magical balance in which he teetered. Another roar shook the ground from the bear, followed by one from a massive tiger.

A quick wave of fear crossed the Boss' face before determination rushed back in. He stepped toward Tim, cutting him off, trying to cover the hole he thought Tim would leave if he got scared and ran. As he did so, he left a gap...straight for Sasha. The creature saw it, saw her, right before Dominicous slid over, covering the path to her with his body.

"Focus, Stefan. Focus on *her*," Dominicous yelled, somehow bracing for that galloping, clawed, grinning monster. Also playing Superman.

"She laid the spell." Toa went down to his knees. He wavered, his brow dipping low over his eyes. Then his eyes closed. Hands met concrete.

The magic in the link whipped wildly, stabbing Charles before ripping away nearly completely. Then back. Toa hung his head, struggling for control. Struggling with a spell so intricate Charles was lost.

The demon lurched toward the Boss. Swirling magic sparkled along the Boss' flexed arms, his sword at the ready. His eyes flashed excitement and wrath ready to be unleashed.

Before he could run forward to meet it, though, leaving Sasha open again, Jonas barreled through. Brawn and snarls, orange sword whirling, the crazy male slashed. The sword cut through the demon hide, eliciting a hissing snarl. A dagger blossomed out of nowhere, Jonas' manic grin one to match that of the demon. Orange blazed and seethed around his arms, turning his body into a weapon. He slashed with them, raking the creature's arm, ripping leathery skin off like peeling a banana.

Sasha stared straight ahead, as if she could still see the demon through a wall of males and fur. Sweat beaded her brow. Her breath came in fast pants. Her thumb stroked her whistle.

"Stefan..." she whispered.

Toa's head bent, panting as well. Dominicous stepped forward to slash the creature but staggered, the magic pulsing in the link swung from one person to the other wildly.

Three wolves and a mountain lion vied for position, trying to close Sasha off. Jameson was there, fighting them back, keeping them from her, but also from the fight. Keeping himself from it as well.

"Fight together!" Charles screamed despite himself, his vision clouding, going dark. Pain screamed at him, stabbing then ripping away, leaving him dizzy in its wake.

Jonas was flung to the side, a gaping hole in his arm where a claw had gouged.

"Stefan..." Sasha pleaded.

"Get her out of here!" the Boss screamed, his sword flashing up, ready for the strike.

"Give her more magic!" Toa yelled back, on hands and knees. "She cannot disengage once the spell is laid. It is too intricate—"

"I can't give to her and fight it off at the same time," the Boss growled. "She'll have no protection! I will trade my life for hers if needed."

"Instead you'll accomplish the opposite!" Toa's head drooped, the magic whipping through the link in hard slashes, pounding Charles, then back toward Toa, then to Dominicous. Painful chaos.

The bear fought to get through. The demon bore down. The Boss' sword came up, as fast as that thing, but before he could lope off an arm, its whole body convulsed.

Its screams cut off at exactly the same moment Sasha fell. Charles dropped his sword in order to catch her, only getting half her body in time, her face scraping the concrete. He cradled her in his arms, half falling on her in a wave of dizziness. He quickly checked for a pulse, his heart in his throat, barely able to see and not caring.

"C'mon, Sasha, be okay," he prayed, his fingers finding the spot on her fragile neck. Her head lolled.

"We've disbanded it," Toa said in a hiss, struggling to get up. And failing.

Charles glanced through the crack in bodies, his vision clearing in a wave as the link dissolved. To an oily black smear across the concrete. The burnt hair smell had turned into a smell of charred flesh.

"If it wasn't for you, would she have made it?" Dominicous asked Toa, shaking like a tall building in an earthquake.

"I was able to cut it off around her spell. Had she had more power and energy, she would've disbanded it quickly and easily. She needed more energy. More power. Only one person could've supplied it—through a blood link."

A beat in her neck pushed back at Charles' fingers. He

sighed in relief as Jonas came running up, blood gushing out of his arm. Behind him loped the huge tiger and a mountain lion.

"She needed you," Toa accused the Boss, still not able to stand.

The Boss stared back, uncertainty warring his blank mask.

"If you won't use your blood link, Stefan, you need to allow someone else to enact one. She cannot be this vulnerable again. You nearly killed her," Toa pushed, anger contorting his face into something out of a nightmare.

"You have to figure out a way to link with her magically," the Boss retorted.

"You think this is over?" Toa shot back, stunning everyone mute with his uncustomary animation. "There'll be more demons. There'll be more perils. Maybe tomorrow. Maybe in a week. Right now, you are her only hope. And you've failed once—what about the next time? What then? Will you let your pride kill her, or will you let someone else help her to live? A blood link is the only way!"

Charles barely had time to witness a flash of anxious defeat cross the Boss' face before he was hobbling up with Sasha in his arms, Jonas helping him stand. He didn't have time for the challenge that was sure to follow—Sasha wasn't out of the woods yet.

CHAPTER FOUR

I was giving Toa a run for his money in the blank stare department. "I'm sorry, come again?"

Toa sat across from me in one of the many rooms in the mansion. Calm and unaffected, as normal, he was trying to convince me to gnaw on his vein. This, to him, was a perfectly normal request.

"With magic like yours, it is sometimes necessary to establish another blood link so you can acquire help in times of...stress," Toa explained for the millionth time.

"You are creating the current times of stress, Toa." I grimaced. The thought of drinking his blood was...revolting. Drinking blood period, when I logically thought about it, turned my stomach. But with Stefan it was intimacy so acute that I felt it the length of my body. It didn't seem abnormal with him. Even the taste was sweet and earthy, pleasurable.

"No, Toa. Just...ew. No. And Stefan would flip."

"Stefan has given his consent."

My flat stare became incredulous. Toa's stare never wavered. "Stefan gave his consent? *Stefan*. The guy that made my bodyguard pee himself when he thought Charles might've laid a hand on me. That Stefan?"

"He realizes that his inaction nearly killed you the other night. You are the most precious thing in his life; it is not asking overmuch to secure your survival. He sees the value in what I propose. He is facing issues from his childhood that shaped him in both negative and positive ways. He's latching onto the negative, clouding his judgment. He has realized this —he is an excellent leader to have done so. It now becomes your obligation to follow through. When he can't help you magically, you will need to turn to another."

"And that's you? So you're going to what, shadow me the rest of my life?"

"We could've lost you, Sasha. Your father, this clan, and our entire organization would've suffered. We need to take steps to prevent that."

"Okay," I waved my hand like I was swishing away flies. "You can cut out the lecture tone and talk normally. You don't have to be all professional about it."

"That is exactly what this is—a professional arrangement. You share a very soft link with Dominicous. He is family. Would it be so strange if you extended that link with the person who shares his blood link?"

"Yes. It would."

We were back to the stare-off. Those ice blue eyes held mine serenely, his hands clasped in his lap. I wouldn't be surprised if he asked for a cup of tea next with a pretty little flowery cup and a saucer.

Still...I had to concede that it had been a close call. I'd been out for two days, so near the brink that only Stefan's blood could revive me. If Toa hadn't disbanded that demon just in time, I wouldn't be sitting here right now. He had saved my life, and now asked to have an easier way to do it in the future.

My stomach turned for a different reason. I hated that Toa was right. That I'd needed Stefan's help with that demon, and he wouldn't supply it. Worse, since that night, three nights ago, he'd been distant. Fear, uncertainty and guilt washed through the link constantly, his emotions raging from one thing to the other even though his face stayed perfectly blank. That demon had triggered old wounds, and now he was trying to shut me out.

But sucking blood from the guy in front of me was a bit extreme. Plus, in what world did I want Toa to feel all my emotions? I might be able to figure out how to cut them off without simultaneously cutting off Stefan's, but I'd still feel what Toa was feeling.

Yuck. No way.

I shook my head. "Why didn't Stefan talk to me about this? He doesn't just give up control."

"As I said, he does not like it, but he does see the value in it. I doubt he wanted to show his weakness by admitting his inabilities."

"You people and your fear of weakness." I blew out a frustrated breath. "Look, either we need to find a different way to share magic, or we just won't. This has gone too far into insanity-ville."

Toa maintained his patient tone as he said, "Stefan is sacrificing on a personal level so that you may have some assurance. Some safety. Will you spit in his eye by refusing?"

Lead settled into my body. The one thing I didn't want to do was let Stefan down for any reason. He'd constantly backed and supported me, sacrificed for me, taken the hard road to stay with me. I owed him some discomfort if it meant he'd rest easier.

I recommenced the stare off, assessing. I really didn't want to. I really, really didn't.

"I'm not convinced he approved this," I muttered.

"What does the link tell you?"

Guilt rode through it heavily, laden with a sense of failure. My heart dropped. He did know. He was sacrificing his dignity, allowing others to see that he couldn't provide for me as he ought, in order to keep me safe. This was terrible, but it was what he wanted.

I shook my head, trying to think of a way out of this. And failing.

CHAPTER FIVE

Stefan sat in the early morning light at the back of the mansion, breathing the fresh air to calm himself. The link with Sasha had winked out a half hour before. He'd felt her doubt, and then she'd muffled their tie, something she did when she was uncomfortable with his presence. It didn't take a genius to know why.

After another fifteen minutes he heard her soft, even pace behind him, making her way to the stone bench on which he sat. He tried not to hunch in on himself as she settled quietly beside him. She didn't touch him as she usually did—not even a glance of the arm.

"So..." She stared out at the budding day, the trees swaying in the chilly breeze of the morning. "You're under the impression I need to share emotion-space with Sir Stares-A-Lot, huh?"

His intestines felt like crawling snakes. "I let you down, Sasha. You could've died."

"True. I could've died a few times since I met you. I've been overextending my whole magical life. And you've always been there to pick up the pieces. I trust you, Stefan. I trust that. You've always kept me safe."

"Not this time."

"To err is human. Even though, you know, you're not actually human. Look, Stefan...tell me what's wrong. Confide in me. Don't just pawn me off on some blondie vampire lookalike because you're too chicken to open up to your future mate. *Please*."

"I just..." How did you tell the love of your life that you weren't worthy of her? That you were a coward. That the male she pledged her life to could not provide for her.

His body hunched.

"Hey," she whispered, swinging her leg over his and sitting on his lap, facing him. She wrapped her arms around his shoulders and pulled his face into her neck. "I know why you did it, okay? I know it was something to do with your parents. It's okay to be afraid, Stefan. We can't be hard all the time. If you can't admit it to me, you'll end up brittle. You don't have to hide that stuff from me."

He shook his head again, emotion he'd been pushing down since he was young bubbling to the surface. "I can't," he pleaded.

"Tell me what happened," she whispered. "To your parents. Confide in me." She hugged him tighter, combing her fingers through his hair. Soft support. Unconditional love such that he could barely remember.

Before he could help himself, it was all tumbling out.

He'd been sitting in the living room as the sun sprinkled through the windows. The knock at the door had echoed down the empty hall. He'd opened it to Jestin, one of the warriors that fought regularly with Stefan's father, scratched and beaten to hell. His face warred with death and sorrow. Lead had settled deep in Stefan's young chest, then, struggling with the dread he'd felt as he read the defeat in Jestin's eyes. The loss.

"Jestin was the only one who lived," Stefan heard himself say. The words sounded hollow. "Two humans called a demon up on the territory line. We were tight with the *Mata* at that time, sharing the coverage of patrolling that line. The demon was a strong one—very strong. It dominated, then killed, those who had called it. The *Mata,* with some of our clan, were supposed to provide the first layer of defense while a team of magic workers tried to cut it down. Tried to banish it."

Stefan shook his head, his body quivering under the petite body of his beloved. "That thing ripped through three people in a split second. Just as the clan was scrambling, trying to get control, the *Mata* took off. Most of the first layer of defense ran like cowards. My father, a fierce fighter and the Second of the clan, did what he could to organize his men, but they weren't enough. Not after the *Mata* had fled. The magic circle was working on it, but that demon took down the line in record time, my father fighting a good fight, but...

"My mother was a green. She had intricate abilities with magic, so she always worked the spells in a Merge with the backing of a few powerful magic users. She couldn't fight— not with the responsibility of casting a spell to take that thing down. She stood where she was, resolute, as, one by one, everyone got chopped down around her. She suffered a hit right before the spell did its job. That thing cut out her midsection. It cut out my unborn sister. Jestin said that when she hit the ground, she was dead. As was the fetus."

Sasha squeezed him hard. Fire burned away his insides, remembering the day he'd heard he was going to be a brother. He was going to be the big protector—his sister's own personal guard unit. His dad had given him a male-to-male talk about the seriousness of his new duty—he would have to be steadfast to her and keep her safe from any danger. His father handed him this personal mission, the responsibility of a grown male.

At the time, Stefan had felt like the most powerful male alive.

It had all been torn away, along with his parents, with each word out of Jestin's mouth.

"Every time I think of a demon," Stefan purged quietly, "I think of losing everything. What if the *Mata* had stayed? The group would've taken some losses, yes. That thing was manic. I might've lost one parent, but my mom would've been protected. She would've made it. I would have a sister. I wouldn't be so damn alone..."

Pain heaved, trying to rip free from the casing he'd stored it in all these years. "I can't protect you, Sasha," he admitted. "I let them die. I should've been there. I was old enough to help. I was already orange by then—orange magic would've helped."

Something inside him broke. His inadequacy of that day raged to the surface, merging with the inadequacy from three days ago.

He didn't know how he'd continue if he lost her. She'd become the most important thing in his life. He would give up everything for her—his clan, his life—everything. And even though every fiber of his person recoiled at the thought of sharing her, if it kept her alive through his failings, then it was worth the torture of knowing another male had a claim on her. He would make sure she lived at all costs; he had no one else but her.

He dug his face into the sweet-smelling skin of her neck and let it all go. Clutching onto her like a lifeline, he purged the fears of losing her, the loneliness of all those years, the desolation after hearing the news spilling out in childlike sobs.

For a wonder, she held on to him. Instead of sneering in disgust at his vulnerability—something the majority of the females in his clan would've done—she held onto him fiercely, as if she was protecting him from his past. As if she was trying to ward away the memories with the warmth of her body.

The lid ripped off their link, her unconditional love and support bleeding through and filling him up. Her worry for him, her devotion no matter what, soaked into his soul. He was ripping at her clothes before he knew what he was doing, stripping off her pants as she yanked at his. Her lips smashed down on his, hot and needy. He ripped off her panties and clutched her hips, pulling her onto his erection, sinking all the way in. Her moan of delight matched his. So tight, so hot, squeezing him in ecstasy.

"I love you," she whispered, swiveling her hips on top of him. His girth slid within her wetness. "You and me, Stefan. I don't need anyone else. I know you'll protect me. When it comes to surviving, I put my faith in you."

Magic whipped around them. He squeezed her tight and held on, thrusting into her savagely, needing her reassurance. Needing her body to back up her words.

They pushed harder and faster, her body crashing down on his manhood. She bent to his neck and bit, hard, her teeth ripping his flesh. He exalted in it, liking the brutality. Loving her fierceness.

The draw pulled through the core of him, directly from his balls. He thrust harder into her, his body slapping against hers.

"Take mine," she murmured, her lips once again on his. "Reinforce the mark, Stefan. Make me yours again. Only yours."

He took her to the ground, his body held tightly within hers. He opened a small cut on her pulse and fastened his lips around it. Her nails dug into his back as he tasted her life's blood, spicy sweet, like her smell. Like her personality. The decadence of her aroma tickled his nose. Her hot sex gripped him.

His world fell over. Out of control and loving it, he pumped harder, his lips against her throat, releasing the special secretion that marked his female as permanently his. He felt her magic pooling around him, her special way of doing the same thing. Mate was a title, marriage was a certificate—what they were doing was a merging of their souls—irreversible.

The deep tingling started at the base of his balls and worked through the base of his shaft. Sasha was moaning, her eyes fluttering, on the edge. He pushed harder, the friction of her body consuming him. As they neared the edge, right on the cliff, he took one more deep draw from her neck.

"Oh my *holy Lord*!" she screamed, her body shuddering, her sex clenching his dick.

He exploded. Emptying into her in a hard gush. He collapsed on top of her, utterly and completely spent.

"Crap," she said, panting. "That was the best yet."

"Uncle."

"What?"

"That's what you always say when we spar and you want out of the various hold I've got you in. Uncle."

"Oh. There is no way I am carrying you."

He huffed out a laugh. "Wimp."

He climbed off and hauled her up. "I take it you didn't take his blood."

Her gaze burned hot with anger. "Don't you ever give your permission for something like that again. You talk to me about that stuff. If there's something wrong, we'll figure it out. If I need to link with someone else, then we'll come to that conclusion together, and we'll hold hands and bear it together. You don't leave me out to dry because you're feeling insecure and vulnerable. Not unless you want a foot up your ass!"

He laughed as he brushed off her back. He loved when she got riled up. "Understood."

"He tried to guilt-trip me. Tried to use you to get me to do it."

"If I thought it was a political maneuver, I wouldn't have let them. But they were worried. No one could help you when I didn't. Sasha, my head isn't on straight. I lost myself to fear." He gritted his teeth, hating to admit this weakness to the one female that he didn't want any weakness with.

Her rage melted into quiet support. She slipped her arm around his back. "I know. And it's okay."

"I'm worried I'll do it again. I hate the word 'worried,' and yet I'm worried you'll need me and I won't be able to clear away the fog. Especially if that..."

Calling Tim a mongrel wouldn't win him any votes at the moment. "Especially if Tim and his..."

She should just stick a knife in his ribs now; it'd be easier. "Especially if the *Mata* are around."

Surprisingly, she laughed. "Wow, that was tough, huh? Being nice? You're as bad as Jonas."

"Jonas lost a parent in that...situation, too."

Her face fell. She nodded.

After they partially dressed they walked back to the mansion in silence, her little hand in his. Finally, he gave in. "I'm not one to...talk about...feelings." He grimaced. "But I'll try to fill you in on...issues, okay? For you, I'll try."

And he'd hate every minute of it.

She laughed again, hugging him close. "*Men*. You bitch and moan about being sick or having a papercut, but tell your significant other about a legitimate problem? Oh my, no, it's more fun to let them worry and fret."

"And then bitch."

"Absolutely we have to bitch! When it's your fault, we have to give a little back."

Chuckling, he swept her up into his arms. As he climbed the stairs, her head lulling on his shoulder, he just hoped he could maintain control for what came. Losing his leadership, and having Dominicous try to rip his arms off, was nothing compared to what he'd suffer if he gave in to fear and it got her killed. He just wished he knew an easy way to navigate through his past. He wished the stakes weren't as high.

CHAPTER SIX

A week after the little demon incident, I stood outside in the failing light with Adnan and his opponent, Claudia. It was the duel I'd initiated before we left to deal with the demon; either Adnan had to beat her fighting-wise, or I had to admit he wasn't as good as I made him out to be.

God, I hoped he was as good as I made him out to be...

Charles stood off to the side, a smirk on his face. He loved watching people fight—because he was an idiot guy—and he loved when I was in a pinch that didn't affect him in any way. This pretty much made his night.

Jonas was off to the other side, totally over this scene, but knowing this needed to happen because I was a loudmouth and made stupid promises. My dallying wasn't improving his mood any, and being that he'd scared a kid on the way out here with just a glance, that wasn't good news.

"Okay, Adnan, here's the deal." I looked him square in the eyes. Young eyes. Belonging to a guy still in school. Who was about to go against a woman who'd been fighting for as long as Adnan had been alive. "You've got to beat her ass so she knows I'm wise and all-knowing, or I have to admit I was wrong. And I hate admitting I'm wrong."

A grin ghosted his lips before uncertainty crept back in. "She's in the Watch, Sasha. She's at her peak."

"You're freaking great at fighting, Adnan. Great." I shook his shoulders a little. "You'll kick her ass, I know it. It's not often I tell a guy to kick a chick's ass, but...give her a bitch-slap if you can."

"You better not get all excited he won and put him in the Watch," Charles said with crossed arms, watching the sneering Claudia as she eyed Adnan. "I'm the youngest brought on. I don't want to give up that title."

"I thought you hated that title?" I shot back.

"Yeah, I do, but with that title, everybody knows I'm the shit."

I scoffed. "Or at least a huge turd."

"Get a move on, human, we have things to see to," Jonas rasped, eyeing the trees like they might come alive and try to stab him.

"No one ever talks to Stefan like this," I muttered to myself.

"He'd rip our limbs off and beat us with them. You'll just shock us," Charles countered.

"In just a minute, yeah. So you have that to look forward to." I honed back in on Adnan. "Okay, ready to kick some butt?"

He flexed his fingers and cocked his head, warming up his neck. Anyone that had ever fought against him usually took a step back at that action. Adnan wasn't super strong in magic, but in fighting, the kid could wipe a smirk off someone's face in a hurry.

I hoped this would hold true for Claudia. She needed to get taken down a peg.

"We have to hit the West Nine after this," Jonas said in boredom as Adnan strolled toward Claudia.

She waited with her hands loosely at her sides, knees slightly bent, and completely relaxed. I had learned that this was the ready position of anyone worth their salt in the fighting arena. Adnan wasn't perturbed.

"Why?" I asked to Jonas as my hands started to tingle in anticipation. I *really* needed Adnan to win this one. "I thought that was a pretty barren place."

"You're thinking of the East Nine beyond the city. The *West* Nine is by Jefferson Park. I gave you the map to study..."

"Yes, Jonas, but Toa gave me a giant scroll on linking. A *scroll* Jonas. He thinks that if I study a five-hundred-year-old document, I'll figure something out. Spoiler alert: I haven't. You know what else I haven't had time for? Geography lessons. Just tell me Jefferson Park if you want me to know what you're talking about."

Charles whistled. "Someone's on shark week."

Jonas and I both shot a scowling glance at the meddlesome dummy. Charles shrugged, "On the rag. Aunt Flo's visiting. Out of commission—take your pick. Although, in extreme situations, and a shower, I don't mind getting a little dirty in the trenches..."

"Ew. Can you not share? It'd really help me out," I begged.

Charles shrugged again as Adnan got within striking range of Claudia. As his right foot touched down, dried leaves crackling with the weight, her hand shot out. Closed fist landed on sharp cheekbone, snapping his head back. His body weight would've followed, landing him flat on his back, but he twisted at the last minute. I caught the briefest of glimpses of his newly split lip before he bounded to his feet, hands out wrestler-style.

"He's quick, but inexperienced," Jonas commented, turning his shoulders toward the fight.

"Slow to get started," Charles intoned. "He'll take a few—"

Claudia's fist landed on Adnan's face again, whipping his head around. A kick made contact with his stomach, bending him over.

"—hits before he finally gets going." Charles shifted, faced screwed up in analysis as he surveyed the fight. "Wait for it, though. He's got talent."

Claudia swept the legs out from under the younger man, rocketing a fist down toward his nose when he hit the dirt. At the last second, Adnan turned, the fist continuing, smacking off the ground. He moved faster than an angry snake, scurrying up and around her. By the time she straightened, his kick landed across her ribs. She sprawled out, face skidding along the dirt.

"C'mon, Adnan," I said beneath my breath, my body tense.

"Here we go," Charles murmured.

"He's not ready for the Watch," Jonas drawled, arms starting to flex. These guys hated when they couldn't join a fight.

"No, not yet. But he's close." Charles flinched as Claudia's foot banged off of Adnan's shoulder. She had a high reach, I'd say that much. "Give him a couple more years and keep him with Sasha and he'll be one of the best."

"Keep him with Sasha? What, does he need a nursemaid?" Jonas snarled.

Irritation bubbled up, but it was Charles that answered. "Bro, where've you been, under a rock? Her special talent is boosting the magic in someone she works with."

"Her special talent?" Jonas spit as Adnan whipped around ninja style, his hands moving so fast Claudia couldn't keep the look of strained bewilderment from her face. He kicked her thigh, jabbed her cheek, and then slashed at her throat. Like a gaping fish, she staggered backward, grabbing her bruised neck.

"Oh shit, yo. He shouldn't have done that. She gets really evil when she's mad." A delighted grin lit up Charles' face.

"What's your special talent?" Jonas asked Charles, glancing sideways at him. "Shitting yourself in glee every time you come?"

"Only if the ladies are into that sorta thing."

"Good god," I groaned. "Why are you guys so gross? I'm in desperate need of girl time. Remind me to call Ann."

Charles laughed. "You know I'm kidding with that comment, right, Sasha? There are certain lines even I won't cross."

I turned to Charles with fisted hands, annoyance bubbling up and overflowing. "Charles, *gross*, okay? I am under a lot of pressure with this council thing in a few weeks, and I don't want to hear about...that stuff. I really don't. Okay? Please?"

"Wow," Charles said under his breath.

Claudia's head tilted downwards like a character in an evil movie. She looked at Adnan out from under short brown lashes. Her eyebrows dipped low over her eyes.

"This just got good, bro," Charles whispered excitedly, his immaturity showing. The guy was bouncing on his feet in anticipation.

Claudia charged, half graceful lioness, half stomping elephant. She rammed a hard blow at Adnan's gut. He blocked, dancing away. She followed, determination and rage warring on her face. She jabbed at him again, followed by a left hook. He took the jab but ducked under the hook, his foot swinging around to clip her on the butt. She was already moving, though.

Red glazed from the tattoos swirling her arms.

"Uh, oh," I muttered. Usually, to spar, Stefan's clan kept magic out of it. When the magic infused the runes and other incantations etched into their skin, their body became a weapon, like a sword or mallet. They could rend and tear as easily as if they had claws.

Claudia was no longer messing around.

"Is this allowed?" I asked in a small voice. "Should I call this off? I don't want Adnan to get hurt."

"He'll be fine," Jonas growled. "He just has to quit dicking around and cash in on her weaknesses."

"He's not as good at identifying that, bro." Charles said while he stared intently. "He hasn't been around the block like you have."

Jonas shifted, his flexed arms coming away from his body, making thick cords of muscle pop out down the length. The gruesome divot where the demon had gouged him was red and puckered, still healing. Although, healing extremely fast. Toa had done something with magic, but wouldn't tell me what. I was to learn useful spells and incantations, like linking, killing, and blocking.

Our priorities were a little different.

A wave of nausea rolled through my stomach at that thought, taking my focus from the fight in front of me. Toa was trying to prepare me for the council with the violent magic. This race of people fought, bled, and challenged each other mercilessly. I was one of them now.

I was nowhere near ready, and Toa knew it.

I groaned.

"What's up, Sasha? Cramps?" Charles glanced away from the intricate and awe-inspiring dance Adnan and Claudia were doing through the trees.

"Charles! I am not on my period!"

Jonas flinched. Charles said, "And you think *I'm* gross?"

"What, because I said period?"

Jonas sent me a disgusted glare.

"Oh really?" I shot back. "You talk about all sorts of disgusting crap, but I say period—stop flinching! Jonas, how the hell can you body-check a demon with a grin and a snarl, but flinch when you hear that word? It's the real word for the thing!"

"Would you stop saying it?" Charles demanded. "Guys don't want to hear about any of that."

I threw up my hands.

Adnan, rivulets of sweat running down his face, had glowing arms in a soft red. He tore at Claudia, raking nails down her arm. He followed it up with a punch, then a kick, stamina holding strong. She was physically flagging, though. Aiming for any weakness she could find. Spells came next, blasting at him, forcing him to try and defend himself magically while she followed up with physical bombardment. Getting dirty to try and counter his limitless energy.

"See, bro?" Charles said, once again analyzing the fight. "Females are much better at multitasking."

"It's why a red is Second-Tier Watch," Jonas remarked, agreeing.

"You guys have tiers?" I asked, flinching as Adnan took a hard hit to the chin. I opened up, immediately fighting the surge of power that rushed me. I felt everyone around me, their strong glow of magic within them, beckoning. Calling. Feeling mine and wanting to join. To take our small fires and create a huge blaze.

I focused on Adnan, knowing he needed a power boost. He was younger, after all. And it's not like I was cheating. Charles did say that if he was with me, and on Watch, he'd be awesome. Well, here was some awesome-sauce.

"Why are you chuckling?" Jonas asked suspiciously.

Ann and I had finally played that joke on him a while back. His butt was glued to the toilet seat for three hours. He was so damn pissed. Afterward, whenever he was an extra big dick, I thought of it and chuckled heartily. Now, every time I randomly snickered, he got suspicious.

"Just marveling at my wittiness." I focused on Adnan's suffocated glow, the pressure of the fight making him tense up, cutting off some of his flow. Like a fan to fire, his magic felt my coaxing, burning it brighter.

His arms flickered, the red getting deeper. Deeper still. Matching Claudia's now as he blocked a physical charge and lashed out magically, the spell jumping the short distance from his skin to hers, something only those stronger in magic could do, and even then, they usually needed the tattoos. I was the exception, as always.

With a growl she wiped her hand through the air, probably shaking whatever it was off. Too late. That stall had Adnan landing two intense kicks, one to her stomach, and one bashing against her thigh. Her feet saw sky. The dull thud of her body sounded like it hurt.

She struggled to get up.

"That's enough," I said in a firm voice. Claudia glared up at me from the ground. "Look, Claudia, you're good, I'll give you that. And you'd keep going, but I'll need you here protecting things when we're gone. I need you healthy for that."

"I could still take him!" she seethed, staring hard.

My hackles rose at the same time as my confidence wavered. I could feel Jonas' stare.

Yes, yes, I know—I'm supposed to lead.

Preventing myself from taking a deep breath, I returned the stare, magic crackling in my body. I felt Stefan through the link, feeling my tumultuous emotions and sending a blast of fire, fueling my courage.

In a breezy, calm voice, I said, "You reached for magic first, needing more than just your fighting prowess. You started to fight dirty first, looking for an edge. And now you're hurt first. What's more, you're worn out. Dead tired. He's a kid—he's got the stamina of one. You're beat, Claudia. Yield."

Her jaw set firmly. Fists clenched and unclenched. Her weight eased over onto her right side. She couldn't prevent herself from wincing.

Her nod was the best feeling I'd had in a long time. Triumph!

Suppressing my glee, I nodded back like it was commonplace and turned to Adnan. "Well done. But you're not Watch material, yet. You have the talent, but you lack the experience. Keep working and someday I'll be proud to welcome you in."

A boyish grin lit up his face. He gave a deep bow. "Yes, Mage."

I fought a grin—I was having a hard time not giggling in delight. With a final nod, and a bursting heart, I turned back to the mansion, and screamed in terror.

CHAPTER SEVEN

*D*ominicous stood off to the side like a phantom, still and quiet, eyes scouring Adnan. His gaze dropped to Adnan's tattoos, still glowing merrily. Then to me.

I did not realize anyone was behind me.

For the first time, I saw Dominicous as everyone else did. He was Stefan's height, cresting six-and-a-half feet, but with a sleeker build than Stefan—not as muscular and robust. He held himself with the same confidence and authority, though, in charge of all things, living or dead, within his world. The master of his universe. The alpha to this warrior species.

It was exactly the same way Stefan looked at things. The two of them were playing a dance of dominance, neither quite sure if they could take the other, and both weighing the odds of losing. And now, with me, both weighing the risks of winning.

As he stood, gazing at me, he had a certain kind of *lean* to him. As if he was always on the balls of his feet with a sword in his hand. As if he was ready to chop my head off at any minute. The cunning and vicious sparkle to his gaze had my warning butt-pucker urging me to either blast him with something awful, or run away really, really fast.

That gaze lasted only a moment, though, retracting so that just warmhearted intelligence assessed me. I let the air escape my body like a punctured tire.

"I second that," Charles muttered. Then, remembering that things just got professional, he gave a slight bow. "Regional."

"Regional." Jonas tilted his head downward, the only other person he showed deference to besides Stefan. It was the only other person that could kick his ass besides Stefan, too, so that made sense.

"I'm sorry to intrude, Daughter," Dominicous said pleasantly, "but I wondered if I might ride with you to the West Nine?"

"Oh. Ah, sure."

He nodded good-naturedly and gestured me in front of him. "Ladies first."

Charles barely contained the snort, the dog.

"How long were you standing there?" I asked as my breath found its way back into my lungs.

"Most of the fight. That young man is one to watch, although not altogether strong with his magic. I'm curious, however. How is it you are able to help others reach a greater potential?"

I briefly explained as we crossed the grounds and entered the mansion, the pull of Stefan guiding my feet. I wanted a glimpse of his handsome face before we left—just in case something nasty waited at whatever place Jonas was taking me. I wanted a goodbye kiss before I faced the next horror.

"Do you have a special skill?" I asked Dominicous. "Charles seems to think his libido is his, and Jonas thinks we're daft. But Stefan has one, and I have one..."

As we walked through the busy hallway, the night just

starting and everyone eager to get to their assigned duties, gazes glanced up and noticed who was coming. The crowds parted for Dominicous in a way they never had for me. Even though I was a mage, I largely had to wind my way through corridors like everyone else. I wanted some deference, if only to own my position, but didn't know how to earn it.

"I could not say if I had a special skill," Dominicous remarked thoughtfully. "I think I have talents, and while they are above and beyond many, they aren't altogether exemplary. You are captured in Fate's web, however. Stefan seems to be, too, whether because of your connection, or because Fate has need of him. Possibly you were given special tools to face whatever will come your way."

We turned a corner and ascended the stairs, the tug getting stronger. My limbs started to tingle and my heart beat wildly. Dominicous said something, but I lost it. I opened the door to find Stefan staring at me from across the empty room. His black eyes, soft with feeling, glittered. The link surged. My chest got warm, love oozing back and forth between us. My lips curved into a smile before I could help myself.

"I felt you coming. I have ten minutes," he said softly, not bothering to glance up and acknowledge Dominicous in the doorway. He'd never liked bowing to a superior, but since he told me about his parents, and shared with me in a way that he hadn't shared with a single person since that day, the subservience of his lesser position had all dried up. The game of risk versus reward had progressed a lot farther than I realized.

Which did not matter at the moment.

"I have ten minutes, too," I stepped into the room.

"Actually, Mage, we should probably—"

I shut the door in Jonas' face.

"Tell me about your victory. I could feel it," Stefan said,

his single-minded focus eating me up as I crossed the room to him.

I reached him in a few steps and slid a hand up his chest. "Later. I need you right now."

He bent in a rush and scooped me up, sitting me on a delicate tea table. His lips found mine, hot and heavy, opening my mouth with his. He slid his hands from my knees to my thighs, pushing my legs open as he did so. His fingers rubbed my apex as his other hand worked at my blouse.

"I love you," he said, tweaking a nipple. A jolt of pleasure shot through my body. It turned to liquid fire, searing down the inside of my limbs.

Suddenly, all I needed in the world was him inside of me.

I yanked at his pants, kissing him in desperation. His hard shaft bobbed out, silky smooth, resting in my palm. I felt along the substantial length until I reached the base. Massaging, I lay back slowly, pulling his huge expanse of shoulder with me to maintain the closeness.

"I need longer than ten minutes," I said in a purr, lifting my butt so he could slide off my black jeans.

"They can wait," he growled, threading two fingers into my slippery sex.

I rubbed back up that smooth skin and tickled the head, eliciting a strangled moan. His thumb found my clit and rubbed in small, slick circles. My hips swung up in ecstasy as I arched back, heat raging through my body.

He slowly laid his body down on top of mine, kissing the base of my neck. Lingering on my heartbeat pounding fiercely. "I can't take blood anymore. Not so close to the council meeting. You need your strength. And you can't take mine—we have to prove you are black, still. If we mix blood, someone will call foul-play."

"Then we better settle for mixing bodies."

Stefan kissed my neck softly, his thumb working faster.

His fingers slid in and out, the sensations reverberating within me.

"Oh, god, Stefan," I breathed, reaching up for his lips.

His fingers slid faster. His thumb pushed harder. Waves of heat washed over me. Coursed through me. Blasted out of me! I moaned as the orgasm ripped me apart, my insides clenching him as my body wracked with shudders.

His lips found mine again, deep and sensuous. He tasted of mint and spice, sweet wine and chocolate. His large body spread my legs wider to admit him. His hand lightly cupped the back of my neck in possession as his weight held me in place.

"You're mine, forever," he whispered.

The tip of his manhood pushed past my lips, and in. Deeper. Stretching me to accommodate him. Filling my body and honing my focus. All the way in he slid until his ends met mine. I moaned into his mouth, not wanting to break the connection of our lips. Not wanting even an inch of distance.

Out he pulled, so slowly. So controlled.

"Whatever happens, I will protect you," he vowed, pushing back in. His hands shook, making a pact with himself. Forcing himself to push past his insecurities and face his fears. For me.

My legs tightened around him, drawing him in. Squeezing him with my interior muscles. Feeling the heat build again. Feeling my body start to wind tighter.

He sighed into my mouth.

The tables squeaked with Stefan's slow, rhythmic thrusts. Controlled, but on the edge. Restrained, but starting to wobble.

My hips thrust forward, feeling his girth within my body. Feeling the friction. High off the contact.

Panting now, sweat coating our bodies, the pace increased. The pressure mounted.

"Oh god," I breathed, squeezing my eyes shut. Tighter and tighter, my core clamped down. His manhood rubbing in just the right place. His thumb and forefinger tweaking my nipple.

"Yes, baby," I exalted. "Yes, baby, please, yes!"

Harder he strove, crashing into me. His body working mine, so deep. Harder. Faster.

I couldn't stop moaning. I couldn't stop...

Electric fire soaked up my body like ink in water. My breath hitched. My world went white hot—

"Oh holy fuuu—" An explosion of pleasure tore through me. I shuddered so hard my teeth chattered.

He moaned into my neck with two last, hard thrusts.

Crack.

Without warning, the legs popped off the table and tipped us over the side. We crashed down to the ground, his big arm ripping me away from the table and rolling me on top of him. When we stopped tumbling, we lay beside pieces of what once was a very expensive tea table from some long-gone century.

"Ow," he grunted. "Those spindly little legs hurt."

"Well, thank ye kindly for calling me skinny." I giggled as I traced my lips along his strong jawline.

"Uh, huh." He winced as he fished out half a table leg and threw it to the side.

"Okay." I kissed him, long and slow. His arms squeezed me, which became awkward when I tried to back off and I couldn't unmash my face from his.

"Mmmkay—weat me oop."

"Mmm?" he asked, his lips curling into a smile beneath mine.

He had my shoulders, but my lower arms were free. I used this to my advantage by punching him in the kidney. With a laugh he let go, allowing me to climb up.

"I have to go on whatever errand Jonas has for me, and you have to go back to being a badass." I shimmied back into my undies.

Stefan turned serious in a blink. His eyes gained an edge. "The site you're going to is old. There's still magic there, which is why they need you, but its use is finished. It's empty. There shouldn't be any danger."

"You hitched when you said 'you.' What don't I know?"

Stefan rose slowly, a lethal predator in his prime.

My libido sparked. "Jeez, I'm getting just as bad as Charles."

A grin tickled Stefan's full lips before he went back to his professional mask. "You need to find a way to link with Toa. He is one of the most powerful whites. More, we can trust him. We *know* we can trust him, which is more than I can say for the other council members. With you and him together, and me to sustain you, we will be a stable powerhouse."

"What about Dominicous? I occasionally get a soft feeling when he's near. Like...kind of like an echo of emotion. Like what I have with you, except extremely, extremely watered down."

"He thinks you two have a soft blood link. If you can..." Stefan's jaw clenched.

"He's family, baby. Or as close to a family as I have. He's not trying to mark your territory." I shuddered with the thought. "Gross."

Stefan's jaw barely relaxed. "After we get you magically linked with Toa, we can try to include Dominicous. This is an extreme amount of power we are talking about—a black, white, and two burnished golds. Not many people can control a link with so much being pumped into it."

"But I thought you guys always had a bunch of people?"

"A group of eight was accomplished once, but it had a green, three reds, three oranges and me. We pulled it in and centralized it. You don't pull. You struggle to keep magic out. Plus...that's just a lot of power with all of us together."

And a lot of power is just what we needed if a stronger demon came along. Which it would, I had no doubt. The one we encountered was just an experiment. The next might be an experiment, too, but I had a feeling it would be a more powerful experiment.

"Okay." I went up on tippy toes to kiss him goodbye. "See you tonight. Love you."

He slapped my butt as I turned away. "Poker tonight?"

"No! I'm sick of losing!"

I pulled open the door to an extremely hostile Jonas waiting right beside the door. Charles stood on the other side of the hallway crocheting, and Dominicous was down the hall a ways, sitting on a plush leather bench against the wall. He had his leg crossed over his knee, focused on an e-reader that he must've borrowed from the uncomfortable-looking guy sitting right next to him, staring at his shoes.

"Took you long enough. Do you not tell him where you need a little finesse?" Charles tucked a crochet hook and a tuft of fabric into his back pocket.

"Crochet?" I asked Charles as Dominicous stood and handed back the reading device. "What about knitting?"

"I can't be carrying around a huge ball of yarn in a bag. People would think I had a purse!"

"Charles...you *knit*. Why not just take that extra step and have a purse, too? What's the difference?"

Charles cocked his head to stare at me. "Are you being serious? A *purse*, Sasha? A male can't be seen with a freaking purse, get real." Charles shook his head as we walked down the stairs.

"Soft is as soft does," Jonas growled with a creased brow. "Want some lotion for your hands?"

"All right Forrest Gump, real original," Charles shot back. "And you never gave back *Scarface*."

I sidestepped the fact that those were *my* DVDs, so I continued to try and figure out Charles. "So you gave up knitting for crotchet in order to be more masculine? Is there something wrong with your head?"

"I crotchet little pieces at a time while waiting for you since you're always on the go lately. So I do the little squares, and then I can fit them in my pocket. I hate being bored, Sasha, you know that. I'm going to make them into a quilt. It'll look good."

"My grandma used to knit," Dominicous said pleasantly. "Mean, vicious old lady. She taught me some great combat moves. She was my favorite relative. I don't think that's how you make a quilt, though."

"I feel like I've just stumbled into the nuthouse," I mumbled.

"Sasha, I wondered," Dominicous continued, "Would you mind dining with me this evening? I'd love to spend some time with you."

A burst of butterflies fluttered through my ribcage. I had so much pressing on me right now, with this counsel coming up, and these demons, and Toa trying to swap fluids, and Stefan's dominance issues—but for all that, I wanted nothing more than to get to know my new adopted father. To finally, after all this time, have a real family. That wanted me. That wanted to adopt me!

"I'd love to," I said quietly, my face getting hot.

"Lovely. What is your favorite meal? I'll have it prepared."

"Burger and fries. She can wolf that down faster than me." Charles peered down the hallway, his eyes starting to lose their happy-go-lucky sparkle. He could be a complete clown in the mansion, but as soon as we stepped outside, his Watch Captain mask clicked into place.

"Anything is fine," I answered, sparing an elbow for Charles. It bounced off his hard lateral muscle. No effect.

"So Jonas," Dominicous said as they turned a corner, fast-tracking toward the front of the house. "What is it you hope to find—"

Dominicous cut off suddenly, his eyes snagged on someone up the hall on the right. A short someone. With a shock of blue hair. She stood in the center of the hallway, staring into a sitting room with a gaping mouth.

"Ann?" I walked up beside her and followed her gaze.

A woman sat back on the couch, completely naked, with her knees dropped to the sides. Another woman, wearing black latex, crouched between spread thighs, going to town on the other woman's lady bits. A man, wearing a freaking catsuit, of all things, knelt next to the woman on the couch, feeding her his large manhood.

"Ah yes, I see you've found the leisure room," I said in a tour guide tone. "I have no idea why, but people seem to gravitate toward this room for weird crap."

Ann turned to me slowly with incredulous eyes. "I knew these people were sexual, but...the *door's* open. And they just go have random orgies? Just, willy nilly, let's have a little sex with a bunch of people in the great wide open?"

"Great wide open?" Charles leaned over us and squinted into the din. "They're in a secluded room. Obviously *you'd* need a nunnery, but here we don't mind having a good time. Although, I think they've gone a little crazy with the costumes. Latex can chafe if you rub against it fast enough."

Jonas stabbed the ceiling with his eyes from a few paces away. If it wasn't for Dominicous, he would've grabbed me by the scruff of the neck and hauled me out of the house already. His eyes had that wild, impatient look that said he was about to snap.

I didn't blame him. This night just kept getting weirder.

As if hearing my thoughts, Ann turned away and said, "Well, this is too strange for me." Before she moved on, though, she couldn't help glancing back into the room. The man was moving around to the latex butt.

She shook her head, ripping her eyes away. "I don't even want to know. He's got a plan, and I don't even want to know."

"He'll probably rip it open with his teeth. She really likes anal stim—"

Ann cut Charles off with a savage punch to his stomach. He wheezed out a breath, trying his damndest not to hunch over.

"I said I didn't want to know," Ann reiterated slowly.

His face burned a light red.

"Sir, we need to get going," Jonas said to Dominicous in a polite snarl.

Dominicous smiled at Jonas agreeably. "Fascinating. I would assume, then, that you would speak to your mage, who is currently in charge of the procession." It was hard to mistake the sharp edge beneath the words.

Jonas slowly turned his wild-eyed stare my way. His teeth ground together and the scars on his neck looked white against his temper-filled, heated skin. He flashed me a *well, come the fuck on* kind of smile that resembled a fanged grimace. My butt tingle sounded for the second time that night. While I did need to learn to lead, I did not need to practice on Mr. Bat-Shit-Crazy right out of the gate.

Nodding diplomatically, I said, "Yes, we need to see to that site. Jonas, lead the way."

"Oh, well, thank you so much, *Mage*." His eyes widened further and his smile looked like a contorted snarl. He whipped around and started stalking down the hall, his hands clenching and releasing as he went.

Dominicous watched him in speculation the whole time.

"What?" I asked quietly as Charles fell way back. If Jonas took his temper out on anyone, it would be him. He was no dummy. Anymore.

"I marvel that Stefan is able to keep that male reigned in," Dominicous noted in a deep voice. "He has a severe problem with authority, and his anger redlines fairly easily."

"Yeah, Jonas is a real treat," I said dourly. Ann snickered behind me.

Dominicous turned his steel-infused eyes my way. "A mage should not have to keep on the knife-point with a member of the Watch. I'm sure someone else would step up and take his place beside you ..."

I waved his concern away. "Jonas has faults in plenty, but there is no one else, besides you and Stefan, that I would want at my back. That guy would—" I shook my head. "He would jab the devil in the eye to keep me safe. He's proved it."

I heard a throat clear behind me.

"And obviously Charles, too. At my back."

The corner of Dominicous' lips quirked as he ingested what I said.

As we stepped outside, I slowed for Ann to walk beside me toward Jonas' Hummer. "How'd you get so far in without someone stopping you?"

"Walked in. No one bothered me."

"They all know you're Sasha's friend. Prudes of a feather flock together." Charles walked around the far side of the vehicle, steering clear of Jonas, who was waiting at the driver's side door, watching them all intently.

"What's that about?" I asked Ann as I hesitated in my walk to the front passenger side door. Regardless of the fact that Dominicous was older than everyone, and the most superior and adult-like, and should probably go in the front like parents were supposed to, as the leader of this crew, that place was reserved for me. I felt awkward.

"When we were at the lodge—the place where you trained in the woods with all the cabins..."

My face lit up in recognition.

"He hit on me. Well, that's not true. What he actually did was ask me if I wanted to have sex. Just like that. Point blank." She put on a dopey expression to mimic Charles. "'Oh hey, animal-human lady— if you're not doing anything, want to have sex? I'm horny—I could do with a lay. Doggy style is fine—I'm not picky.'" Ann threw a glare into the car.

"So what'd you do?" I laughed.

"I punched him in the nuts, obviously!" Ann scoffed, trying to hide the smile. "He's hot, though—if he put a little time and effort into it, I might've."

She lowered her voice to a whisper, glancing at the driver's side where Jonas waited with his forehead against the steering wheel. "Jonas hasn't freaked out that I'm going. Is that because of Dominicous?"

I matched her tone—it was best not to aggravate the guy any more than he already was. "He's so mad right now that he has to have some quiet time or he'll explode. If it was just me, he'd rant and rave and argue. If Dominicous or Stefan is around and he's like this, he simmers in acute aggression. Word of advice: Don't badger him until he calms down."

"I'm not suicidal," she said, scurrying into the car. She'd sit between the two guys in the back.

I headed to my spot and climbed in, with Dominicous getting in as well. Once we were all settled, Jonas took his head off the steering wheel, flashed me a look promising pain, and jerked the ignition, starting the car.

"Sasha," Dominicous spoke up over the roar of the motor. You would almost believe he was a gardener of beautiful flowers rather than a lethal predator. "Did you plan to ask Stefan to dine with us, tonight?"

"Uh…" I hadn't had much time to think about it.

"I would encourage you to bring him, if you like," Dominicous continued. "I rarely get to see the pair of you outside of a work capacity. Dropping titles for a family dinner would be a luxury."

A shiver went up my back, both because he said family, and because Stefan had been dropping titles off and on, anyway. Jonas' lips quirked, probably thinking the same thing. Right before he shoved his phone in my face.

"Jonas, I'll ask him later," I mumbled. The man was starting to be as overbearing as Charles.

"He has a million things to prepare and see to. He might have to rearrange his schedule." The phone inched toward my nose.

"What are you, his secretary? I'll ask him later."

"Just text him," Ann helped from the back. "That way it won't be embarrassing asking honey-do-dah for a date with your new dad in front of other people."

"Yes, thanks for saving me all that embarrassment, Ann," I replied in a dry tone.

"No worries."

I pushed Jonas' meaty hand away from my face as we pulled up to Jefferson Park, bringing out my own phone and whipping off a text real quick. I figured I'd leave it open—I'd ask if he wanted to go, but tell him it was totally fine if he didn't. Because he definitely wouldn't—he'd be worried he'd finally start a fight…

The night pressed against the windows, the waning moon not giving us much to see by. And by 'us,' I really meant me, because even Ann had better night vision than humans.

I climbed out of the car into the stillness of midnight. The lush night harbored a chill that had me pulling my hoody tightly around my body. Large oak trees reached overhead, their leaves littering the ground, a blanket of browns and blacks, the brilliant colors of fall muted in the darkness. Dominicous stepped out beside me, standing close, his body poised, his pleasantness shed like a second skin. His eyes scanned the area, his arms glowing lightly.

Ann gracefully stepped around the car, followed by the stern and serious face of Charles. Last came Jonas, his hulking shoulders and thick arms lightly flexed, prepared for the anti-Christ as a normal course of his duties.

Something felt off about this place. Some weird energy was poking at me. It was like the equivalent of someone swishing the very ends of my hair. Disturbing.

"Something's not right," I said slowly, turning toward a black patch between two monstrous oaks. "I feel..."

Charles stepped up beside me, a hand on my shoulder. "Don't go chasing demons, Sasha. If something pulls at you, you shout that shiznit out."

"There ain't no demons." Jonas stalked by, his glare flaying Ann as he passed her. "Follow me."

He led the way through the still copse of giant trunks, the ground bumpy with fallen acorns. The thick hush of the night hovered, sound strangely deadened. Another few steps had us nearing the edge of the plant life, the tableau opening up into a flat grassy soccer field with two skeletal frames of soccer goals hunkering in the distance. Beyond that, a playground spread out, shadowed and deserted.

"Mage, I ask permission to assume control of the battle tactics," Dominicous said officially.

The guy was the Regional, for Christ sakes. He didn't have to ask for anything, especially of an inexperienced mage. But this was a *teach Sasha how to lead session*, so I let it go.

"Yes, that would be helpful, thank you," I replied, feeling that weird magical presence prickling my skin. Like someone tapping me on the shoulder softly, but when I turned, all I found was empty air. It unsettled me. Whatever hovered here was not natural, whispering without sound. Blowing on my face and then disappearing.

"Okay, I'm going to feel this out. You guys should all give me some space. Last time, my magic woke up something awful." I let the rush of the elements fill me as the guys and gal drifted to the side, even Ann in predator mode, filling in as one of the team. Jonas, for a wonder, let her.

Dominicous gave instructions, but I didn't hear him. I let my focus hone and my magical feelers drift out, covering the area in a thin fog of black. I could feel the remnants of something magical lingering. Like a rope with the frayed ends singed, the magic had been cauterized. Whatever spell was weaved originally had been snuffed out.

I wandered forward, through the trees, ducking branches and brushing leaves away from my face. The unsettled feeling got stronger, my skin starting to itch. I emerged through a wall of branches and found myself in a small clearing, closed in by trees. A rough circle scarred the trampled grass, the bent and broken blades shimmering with dew in the faint moonlight. My eyes caught a symbol edged in the thick bark of a tree at the edge of the open space.

"A good ol' pentagram," I mumbled quietly. "As if that wouldn't give it away."

The magic here lay across the ground in a twisted blanket of decay. Spells had been laid, woven and coaxed to life, but whatever came of it had fallen apart. Fallen apart, but not disintegrated back into nature, as elements naturally did. The magic user was working with bad juju on this one. Twenty bucks said he then moved on to experiment in a warehouse.

"Well, at least there isn't a demon to deal with. That's something."

"What's that, sweet thang?"

I started at the unfamiliar voice. To the right, a man wiped draping branches out of the way and stepped into the small clearing. I flinched as his foot stepped on the line of the circle, my mind registering that he'd interrupted a barrier, my logic late in mentioning that it wasn't a barrier anymore.

"What are you doing here all alone?" His lust-filled notice raked down my body, blossoming fear and a crawling sensation where they lingered. "Don't you know there are bad things that go bump in the night?"

Another man, slightly larger and twenty pounds heavier, stepped out beside him.

"Well, that's lucky," the second man said, his gaze traveling the same path. It lingered on my crotch. "I thought we would have to smoke a joint alone. Looks like we have a party."

A sneer worked up the first man's face. "Yes we do, and plenty to go around."

My breath started to come out in fast pants. My fingers itched for my rape whistle. My warning butt pucker said *run!*

Once again, logic was late to the party.

Sasha, you moron, you have magic, remember?

I also had huge guys within screaming distance. Not to mention a mountain lion with a terrible sense of humor about being hit on. Yeah, I was safe. These guys, however...

I tried to quell the rising tide of panic, but a lifetime of knowing, with certainty, what happened when a woman got caught in the middle of the night, in a remote location, with two thugs that probably had arrest warrants, battered at my rational mind. With a thumping heart, I thought about what to do first—blast them with magic, or just call for Dominicous.

Before I could settle on a course of action, though, a third giant man stepped into the clearing. This one came with corded muscle running the length of his body, was coated with silver lines of battle scars, and had eyes brimming with undelivered death. Jonas. My butt puckered for an entirely different reason.

Jonas had just found a target for his building bad mood.

"Look, guys, this is a bad spot for you," I warned.

"Is that right?" the nearest guy asked, stepping closer. I could see his body tightening, ready to make a grab for me. Waiting for me to run.

"No, seriously..." I pointed at Jonas.

The larger guy in back glanced back quickly, did a sweep right past Jonas with his gaze, and came back to me with a smirk. "I fell for it. But you didn't run... Feeling lonely tonight? We can help with that..."

Damn logic and its constant dilly-dallying. Of course they couldn't see Jonas. I'd spent a lifetime hiding the fact that I *could*.

"Right, okay, you guys—"

The guy in the front stepped forward, cutting me off. Immediately a spell found its way to my lips—I had no idea which one, but I was pretty sure it would be awful. My reflexes were fast, but never pretty.

As the words formed, the thug's hand reaching for me, Jonas rushed into the clearing. However fast I was, he was lightning.

He snatched the thug's hand out of the air and whipped it around. He grabbed the man's throat and held him still while he bashed a fist into the thug's face, all his force behind it. The man's nose burst, blood gushing down his face.

"Ease up, Jonas. Let the cops have him," I bleated.

His face a terrifying mask of rage, Jonas reached back to let another punch fly...but hesitated. His elbow, in the air, ground to a halt. He was defending one of his own, for his Boss, and every instinct in his body said *kill*. But I'd said stop.

"*Ease up,*" I said again, injecting a whip crack of command into my words.

Like cement drying, Jonas' arm quivered where it had stopped. He exhaled slowly, shaking, holding his temper at bay. Following my command.

With a roar of frustration and awesome show of strength, he picked the guy up by his neck and nuts, and bodily threw him to the side. A splash of limbs landed and tumbled within the leaves, their owner long since knocked out.

Charles stepped into the clearing, watching the last remnants of limbs tumbling. Dominicous stepped in next to me, eyes surveying the magical site.

I had just witnessed Jonas taking it easy on someone. Picking them up and throwing them ten feet was him doing the right thing... His being on my side was a blessing and a curse at the same time. I had to remember to ask Stefan if he felt the same way.

A manic grin spread across Jonas' face as his crazed gaze fell on the other stranger, currently standing with eyes so round they looked like golf balls. "This is your lucky day. Mage says I can't kill you."

Jonas heaved a sigh, letting the last of his rage simmer down. "Well, fuck it."

He stepped forward. The man cowered down, throwing up his hands. I could just see his face peeping out, staring up at Jonas with wide, fear-filled eyes until a dreamy haze settled over his features. As Jonas reached him, the man had a pleasant, lust-filled smile.

"You're not going to—"

Even as I said it, Jonas put a hand on the man's shoulder and pushed. The man fell to his knees, eagerly reaching for Jonas' zipper.

"I either need to beat someone to shit, or get a load off," Jonas growled, the anger still lurking at the base of his words.

"Okay, no, I don't care that he was going to do that to me —that's not what we're about—" A light touch on my shoulder stopped me.

"Your human sentimentalities between right and wrong as regards to sexual endeavors are different than ours," Dominicous said softly. "To lead this clan, you have to understand this clan. You stopped your protector from killing, even though it was his right since his mage was assaulted. And you could stop him now, but denying him his every instinct will make him revolt. And this male, in particular, needs no pushing on that score."

Dominicous waited a moment for that to sink in.

"That man should be killed," he continued in a reasoning tone as the man eagerly took Jonas out of his pants. "Instead, you have spared him. Think of the charity you have shown."

"So, wait," Ann stepped through the trees with a sour expression. "You're pissed because that dude was going to rape Sasha, but you're totally fine when Jonas does it back?"

"But he likes it," Charles countered in exasperation. "Jonas isn't even touching the guy. Look. That guy is all over it. Seriously, humans feel like the masters of the universe the next day. Do you know how many porns feature this kinda thing? A. Lot. Let me tell you. Girls dig this whole submission thing, too, don't say you don't. I snooped around Ann's room when we were in the cabins—I know what she reads."

"You did *what?*" Ann screeched, losing her calm demeanor.

"Reconnaissance. Romantic comedies didn't work, so I figured I'd check out the reading material. Kinda dumb, though. If I said some of that stuff to you, you'd punch me in the head. You human women have a screw loose—even the ones that get real hairy, like you."

"That is a valid point, Ann, regarding mind-altering in order to control for personal gain," Dominicous said patiently, ignoring the sudden tension between Charles and

Ann. "You are making it with the wrong person, however." Dominicous looked at the pentagram on the tree. "This is the culture, right or wrong. This culture cannot be changed overnight. They have always thought themselves better than humans. They have also held a grudge, since humans are still dominant. Sasha can tell you the stigma a human carries. But these points are extremely valid, and probably need further investigation. The clan needs someone to lead the way. Slowly. Gradually."

Ah. Yes. Let the sore thumb in the group sort it out. That'd really help my chances of fitting in. I couldn't help my scowl.

Well, at least some people viewed the situation logically.

"Fine." I prevented myself from watching as the man jumped up and turned around. This had happened before, sure, but my world had been blown apart then—nothing seemed real, and I hadn't had time to digest before more crazy happened, like *Dulcha*. I wasn't so lamb-eyed anymore, though. Can't change it in a day, fine. I prevented killing today, and I'd prevent this weird crap down the road.

"At least do it somewhere else!" I shouted at Jonas, losing my control. I threw Dominicous a glare as if to say, that's a battle I plan on picking every time, culture or no.

Dominicous nodded once, unperturbed.

"You not going to dive in?" I heard Ann ask of Charles with an accusatory tone. "At least then you'd stop pestering me for sex. And spying."

"I will never stop pestering you for sex, and no. Sasha makes my life hell when I do things she hates. I can abstain," Charles sniffed.

Ann scoffed behind me, but a glance revealed a small tweak in her lips. A person just couldn't stay mad at Charles. The guy was a clown at the best of times.

"Okay," I said softly, careful not to step into that circle.

Nothing would happen, but ... just in case. I traced the pentagram with my pointer finger, the deep groove in the scratchy bark giving me a pleasant tingle through my fingers.

"That's odd," I said, squinting through the darkness to try and make out the lines more clearly. Obviously my logic was still on hiatus. "Does anyone have a lighter or something? I can't see a damn thing."

"What happened to the lighter you use for your crack pipe?" Charles asked as patted his pants pockets.

"Charles, stop trying to be funny. You're no good at it," I retorted in a wispy voice, feeling along the bark with my palms.

Ann stepped forward, the *kush* of her feet on the grass in the circle giving me goosebumps. She held up a lighter, her eyes always on the move.

"You smoke?" I asked as I grabbed the warm plastic.

"Nah. But I hang out with a guy that does. Ever notice that smokers never seem to have a lighter on them?"

"What guy?" Charles asked suspiciously. "I'd hate to think you're giving it up to someone else when you have me to choose from."

I couldn't see her eyeroll, but I was sure it happened. At least he had someone new to badger besides me.

Although, Charles had a point. Ann and I weren't besties yet, but we were working on it, and that was something girls needed to chat about. I scribbled a mental note in my memory.

The click of the lighter echoed in the hush of the night. Flicking light revealed that the scratch in the bark was light brown at the bottom, indicating this was a recent carving. I said as much as I glanced down at the circle. The grass had moved and shifted, as living things do, overlaying a circle that must have been drawn at least a few weeks ago.

"But why would he come back and scratch the pentagram?" I asked as I turned back to the tree. "That doesn't make sense. And the feel of that symbol is all tingly and lovely. Everything else in the air is..."

"Rank," Charles helped, letting an exaggerated shiver roll through his shoulders.

"I can't feel the magic, but it does smell off. Also smells like..." Ann kneeled to the circle, eyes scanning the now empty area. "I'd bet something was killed here. Something small."

"Something nobody would miss," Jonas said as he strolled back into the area. He only looked mildly more relieved.

"What'd you do with him?" I asked in a testy voice I couldn't help.

"Wiped his memories, threw his clothes in a tree, and sent him stumbling through the park naked. I hope he gets pneumonia. He signed his death warrant when he went after you." Jonas flexed from head to toe. He cracked his neck.

"Do you kill small animals, too, psycho?" Ann asked offhandedly.

"Only human ones," Jonas growled back.

"Look here." Dominicous extended his finger to a few scratches in the bark, further up from the pentagram. "Someone of my height drew these. They look older. The weather has worn the freshness."

I handed him the lighter so he could hold it up. They were characters.

"Runes," Dominicous said to my stare. "But I don't know what they mean. Toa would know."

Of course he would.

"Well, this happened before that warehouse thing. And being as though there wasn't a mass riot, I'd assume this attempt at bringing a demon through didn't work," I surmised, stepping away.

"Bringing it through what, exactly? A portal?" Ann asked, giving me room.

I bit my lip, thinking. "From wherever they exist when it isn't here. We should consult Toa."

I hated that hint of sullenness in my voice. Dominicous did me a favor, and kept himself from nodding.

"Okay." I dusted off my hands and looked to Jonas. "Anythi—"

"Incoming," Charles interrupted in a low voice. Before I could even open my mouth to ask a question, he rushed across the small clearing, threw a thick arm around my middle, and bodily carried me into the treeline. He dropped me against a trunk and stood over me as Dominicous melted in beside me. Jonas drifted toward the opposite side of the clearing, his tattoos glowing faintly right before the shadows seemed to reach for him, pulling him into their bosom protectively. Ann was beside me a moment later, her brow dancing on her face as she processed smells. It was her "huh?" face.

She showed that face to Charles all the time. But then, we all did.

"Smells like women," Ann said softly, the sound barely tickling my ears. "Fresh scents, fragrant, floral soaps..."

"Why would women come here so late—"

"*Shhhh!*" Charles hissed in my ear.

"Humans can't hear as well as you," I softly whispered back.

"Might not be human," he answered.

I felt a light touch on my shoulder. Dominicous telling me to shut it.

We waited in silence as the bodies drew near. Footfalls were the first thing to reach my ear. Someone pounded the ground with decisive, no-nonsense steps. Fabric swished, like tracksuit pants. Something dragged, tinkling and jingling.

"Human," Charles assessed. "Sounds like a pack of elephants in a lightning storm."

Where did he come up with this stuff?

Dominicous shifted, his body melting down into a pose of patient relaxation. Jonas shifted across the way, too, only his was in irritation. He obviously had other things he wanted to do tonight. We were not great with time management.

A moment later, four women walked cautiously into the clearing. The woman in the lead, wearing a thick gray skirt and black, long-sleeved shirt tucked in, was the force behind the thumping feet. Probably five-foot-eight and pushing sixty, her large bosom took up her whole chest, straining the effectiveness of her bra as they reached for the ground. She broke the tree line and paused, hands on hips, surveying the surroundings like a groundskeeper might notice his freshly mowed lawn. Behind her skulked a small woman in her early thirties, thin and mousy, sporting glasses held together with tape in two places. She held a Taser in one hand and pepper spray in the other.

She wouldn't have been my optimum choice for a battle unit.

Behind them crowded a pair of twins, which had Charles perking up considerably. If it wouldn't draw attention to our hiding place, I would've punched the idiot. Pudgy with round faces, each had a smile and a splash of freckles. They looked around like they were waiting in line at the fair.

"Okay, ladies, let's set up," the woman in the lead said, glancing down.

Each woman spread around the circle, not one of them stepping over the now disturbed line. One of the twins dropped a small satchel, the burst of metallic tinkling making the mousy woman jump and crouch, weapons of destruction aimed at the disturbance.

"No one's here," the leader said, waving away the mousy attack unit. "You can calm down."

With a last glance around, the mousy woman slightly relaxed, hunching just a bit more in bad posture as she settled to the ground cross-legged. Soon everyone else joined her, each shifting and moving until they found a comfortable spot.

"Okay," the leader said, straightening out her skirt with firm pats. "Focus, now."

Charles sighed softly and leaned his forearm on the tree over me, getting comfortable. His hard chest pushed into my face, squishing my nose and having me gasping. I grabbed skin in my two fingers, squeezed, and twisted for all I was worth. It was a pinch to tell the masses about. They probably used it in the Spanish Inquisition.

Charles grunted and backed off quickly, the slide of his skin on bark permeating the space. The heads of all four women snapped toward us.

Oops.

It was all his fault, obviously.

The mousy girl raised the pepper spray, her face pointing to the area between Dominicous and Charles. In other words, between the two trees. Time tumbled by, soaking the area in silence. A dry leaf clicked off another dry leaf above us, like miniature skeletons dancing. Still the women stared. Still we froze.

What were we all waiting for?

Jonas put his hands on his hips on the other side of the clearing.

Oh, good, I was developing Jonas' impatience. Fabulous.

"Did you hear that?" one of the twins asked into a hush with an unlit lighter hovering over a corroded silver candleholder. She had forgotten about the candle part of the whole affair.

"Are we not all staring in the same direction?" the leader

asked with a verbal rolling of the eyes. "But I can't see anything, and there've been no other sounds, so..."

The pepper spray dropped a fraction.

"Well?" the leader prompted.

The lighter clicked as the twin got back to business. "Oh." She went rummaging through the bag for the missing candle.

"Should we not head out?" Dominicous whispered, the words barely reaching my ears.

"Yes, but...just a second. I want to see what they're up to." My gaze was riveted to the leader, stretching out. Loosening her joints. For what? An intense game of thumb war? I'd bet these people scratched that pentagram—I had to know why.

CHAPTER EIGHT

"Boss, something's come up."

Stefan looked up from the desk where Sasha's text message from earlier lit up his phone, letting him know of a potentially uncomfortable dinner later that night. Just this once he'd love to say no to her. He hadn't been able for the deference he was supposed to be showing the Regional lately, grinding the two of them nearer an altercation. But that woman had him by the balls. All she had to do was bat her eyelashes, or pout, or smile, or—hell, text message, and he couldn't help immediately bending to her whims. He'd turned soft with regards to her, but...

No. End thought there. She'd turned him soft.

Stefan unconsciously flexed. Jameson stood in the doorway, cell phone clutched in his hand.

"What is it?" he asked his second in command.

Jameson stepped into the room, the dim light reflecting off of the sword hilt at this back. "I just got word from the West Three. We've got another one."

"Grade?"

"Low. Probably not much better than a Dulcha. It's confined in a circle. Creator is nowhere to be found."

A low-powered demon meant Stefan's magic, and that of his more powerful Watch, would be enough to dispatch it. He wouldn't have to involve Sasha.

Stefan stood from the desk in one quick, fluid movement. "Who else knows?"

"Some humans found it. They were sitting around, staring at it when we showed up."

"Their memories?"

"Wiped. They were relocated."

Stefan nodded, feeling adrenaline fill his body for what he knew lay ahead. He rolled his shoulders and shook out his hands. No distractions this time. No mangy animals, Regional, or fear for Sasha. Just him, his Watch, and his sword. It was time to test his resolve.

A grin worked onto his face as he hefted his sword and some battle leathers.

"Should I contact the mage?" Jameson asked in a level voice.

"No. Get a crew together and meet me out front. Ten people should be fine, with an additional ten on call if something goes wrong."

Jameson nodded, phone already at his ear.

Stefan brushed passed his Second and out into the hall. A younger female startled at his appearance and shuffled out of the way with a red face. He strode powerfully toward the weapon room. Members of his clan always gave him plenty of space, but now everyone jogged out of the way, sensing his mood and reading his body. It was time for battle, and the wise got scarce or joined in.

After gearing up, he nodded to Tace, a stout male with spikes on his shoulder piece, before heading toward the front of the house. At the end of the hall by the door waited the bleached blond head of a huge pain in the ass.

"Guards are generally on the *outside* of the building," Stefan growled as he neared, Tace right behind him, ready for war.

Toa didn't so much as blink. "Were you planning to alert the mage that a magical anomaly dictates her presence?" he asked in his quiet tone.

"A nothing of a demon doesn't dictate anything. I can handle this just fine."

Toa glided from the wall and followed Stefan out the door. It took everything he had not to knock the meddlesome male through the wall he'd just been resting on.

"So, you did not tell her," Toa accused conversationally.

"Correct. She is otherwise engaged."

"I see. What about the Regional? Does he not deserve to know what goes on in the territory he is currently occupying?"

A flash of rage swept across Stefan's consciousness. He stopped suddenly, muscles flexed. His eyes bore into Toa, having the other male's back snapping straight and a foot retreating, his brain no doubt begging to find somewhere safe to hide. "This is *my* territory. I will run this territory as I see fit. If you keep meddling in my affairs, I'll silence you, regardless of your higher level of magic. Is this clear?"

Stefan had to hand it to the male, his gulp wasn't nearly as loud as some.

"I will be accompanying you, of course," Toa said in a calm voice, despite the sheen of sweat that coated his forehead. "I will fill in for your mage."

"I don't need you." Stefan commenced walking, pushing through the door and out toward Jameson, standing beside a sleek sports car. Tace followed him like a shadow, waiting for directions.

"It is not a question of *need*," Toa said as he drifted along beside Stefan. "I want to analyze the spell. I need to know more about the magical properties behind this. Whoever is calling these demons, he is not doing it with the same chants and old magic the humans use. He is working at it a different way. Being that it is one of our kind, I can figure out his reasoning. With study, I can get ahead of him. I can find him and take him to the council."

Stefan took a silent, deep breath. It was always analytics with this guy. Thinking and pondering and twittering about it. He had no idea how Dominicous, a man of action like himself, could deal with it. But Toa did have a point. Knowing the enemy was always the first step. Knowing, finding, and then killing.

"Stay out of my way," Stefan growled as the car door was opened for him. "I'll give you time to look around before we kill it. After that, you can have all the time you need."

He turned back, staring at the icy blue eyes with fire. "But everything you learn will be shared. You will dissect everything with Sasha or myself. No secrets. Don't forget within which territory you reside."

"This is a dangerous road you are walking," Toa replied in a low voice.

Stefan intensified his focus until Toa's gaze hit the ground. He hated that he had to keep reminding the Regional and his mage that Stefan ran this territory. Deferring to a higher power was tolerable for short periods of time, but these two had overstayed their welcome. Alphas didn't like to share, and Stefan liked it less than most.

They arrived at the site: a deserted parking lot at a closed-down roller rink. On the side of the building, hunched within the shadows, moved a creature about the size of an average human male, confined within invisible walls, barely hanging onto its physical shape. It stared out at Stefan's gathering clan, huge teeth protruding from black lips and gums. Saliva dripped out of its mouth and fell to the ground in strings.

"It greatly resembles a *Dulcha*," Stefan noted as Jameson stepped next to him.

"*Dulcha* register at about a nine or ten—the lesser powerful end of the spectrum—depending on the magic used. This is probably a seven or eight. Small animals were sacrificed in the ritual," Jameson conveyed.

"But it *was* a ritual?" Toa asked, focusing his unblinking stare on the glistening eyes and grotesque face of the demon.

Jameson concurred, "From what we can gather, it has all the elements of the warehouse. The pot, the fire, the blood sacrifice, the containment circle…"

Toa stepped closer, a white haze drifting across the ground toward the demon, his magic picking up clues. "He'd called too powerful of a demon the last time. It didn't want to stay put. The caster wasn't ready to battle wills, so he ran. This time, in order to continue practicing, the caster scaled way back. He called a lesser demon. A lap dog. Oh yes, I see…"

An orange light blared into existence around the demon, a circular, magical cage.

"Intricate," Toa droned, talking mostly to himself. His eyes had lost focus. His magic spread around the area in a pale white glow. "The spell is tied off. It doesn't want for more power. Stronger in construction, this time. Fine details. Someone working on his craftsmanship."

Toa straightened up, ignoring the horrible rasp coming out of the demon's mouth. His gaze hit Stefan's. "The wielder of this spell is getting close. This spell is polished; sophisticated. I imagine the chants for the various demonic power levels have been mapped out. The confinement is water-tight. The workmanship is *just so*. Yes, he's not far now. It won't be long before he calls a nasty demon. One, maybe two more tries, and he has something that will bend to his will."

Ten warriors, armed in leather, knives and swords, tattoos glowing and eyes fierce, waited silently for the fluffy, white-haired mage to finish prattling on about his findings. Adrenaline from the battle to come raged through their blood, needing action. Needing release. The scene could be dissected after the demon was dispatched.

"Do you have what you need?" Stefan asked with iron in his voice. He didn't need to follow the question with a command to move. Toa was already taking himself to the rear of the warring party.

"Do you plan to link?" Toa asked with a rigid back and somewhat raised chin. "Or are you planning to do this all on your own?"

Stefan jerked his head to his Watch. Understanding the silent command, they spread out in a circle surrounding the demon, swords flashing to life.

"This demon is nothing. It's sport." Stefan ripped his sword out of the holster, the blade blaring burnished gold with a white frost. "It's practice for my Watch."

Stefan could barely hear Toa sniff. "Well, I'll just wait near the cars then. Since you claim to have this covered."

The white mage wasn't used to being a spare tire. Stefan smirked. It was good for him.

Stefan called the elements, filling himself with more air and fire than the other two. He let his magical feelers pick at that spell surrounding the demon, getting an idea of it. Finding the weak points. And then noticing a big, magical "pull here" tab to unravel the whole thing. Organized, logical and effective—if the person responsible turned out to be anyone besides Andris, Stefan would be shocked.

Stefan had spent a few hours interrogating Trek after they'd captured him, who was holed up in the basement of the mansion waiting to go to the council and get his punishment. The caped buffoon had a lot of interesting information to divulge, like their extensive gathering of humans to make *Dulcha* and for draining blood for power. And Andris' teaching, alluding to him being the mastermind behind all their dealings thus far—something Stefan had always suspected. Most importantly, their collecting of ancient human texts about calling demons and ruling the world.

The latter made Stefan chuckle. Andris had been telling tall tales to the naïve and greedy white mage—to manipulate him, no doubt. Ruling the world only existed in storybooks, and only lasted for a short time before the "good guys" rolled through and tore the mantle from the villain. Trek was an idiot, but an idiot with golden information.

"Prepare yourselves," Stefan commanded in a low tone.

Through the link he could feel Sasha, the hum of her daily activities creating nothing more than small mood fluctuations. Safe.

He bent his knees and breathed through his mouth. *Here we go.*

A magical tug had the containment spell dropping away, the confinement suddenly thrown wide. The demon within stood still for one moment of uncertainty, noticing the disappearance of the cage. The next second, it was action.

With a scream like a dying cat, the creature tore out of the circle, heading right. Silvia whipped across the cement as clawed feet scraped. It dove for a pocket of air between Jameson and Sid, not aiming to fight or kill, just to escape. Strange.

Jameson's pale gold sword whipped up, slashing across its middle. The creature bellowed, sliding away and running the opposite direction. Flesh flapped, its back flayed away from the rest of its body. A pungent smell of rot wafted by Stefan's nose as it passed, screeching.

Tace met it this time, his sword slashing a thigh. The bright red blade seared a stringy leg, making the thing stumble and change direction, this time right for Stefan.

Memories flashed. The knock at the door, slow and solemn. The empty dining room table, dinner getting cold. A tear, unabashed, falling out of Jestin's eyes as he told Stefan the news. Nightmares. Decades and decades of nightmares; going up against a demon like this and failing. Claws ripping into his father. Teeth cutting out his mother's throat. A baby dying. Stefan curled in a ball while the beast ravaged his family.

As the memories crowded his brain, sweat covered his body. He squeezed the hilt of his blade. Images of blood clouded his vision. Spilled blood. Flying blood. Blood splashed across the cold dirt.

Pressure condensed his chest. A dull roar rang in his ears.

Screaming. His parents screaming.

"No!"

Almost unable to feel it, he slashed. A claw came sailing passed his head. He ducked with plenty of time, faster than this worthless creation of death. He struck downward with his sword, slicing off an arm. His other hand brought up his knife even as his eyes stung. The memories, so fresh, suffocated him.

"Die!" he heard himself say, his dagger piercing the face. He let go of it and stepped back, quick sword work slashing and hacking, cutting chunks out of masticated flesh. Parts dropped away. The thing screeched and howled. Still he worked, vision gone red. Pulsing pressure in his ears. His mother screamed in his dreams.

"Please, *no*!"

"Boss."

Panting, lost, he stabbed and stabbed. Over and over. Until it was just a lump of burnt flesh on the ground.

"Boss..."

Dirty and sweaty, Stefan stilled his body. Dragged himself out of a life's worth of nightmares.

"You got it, Boss?"

As Stefan's vision cleared, he found himself looking up into the logical brown eyes of his second in charge. Jameson held out a hand, resolute, asking to help Stefan up. Stefan's gaze swept the ground, the lumps at his feet no longer recognizable. Blood smeared his body, sinking into the grooves of his muscles.

"I didn't realize these things bled," he said as he allowed Jameson to help him up.

"It's the blood sacrifice. They don't bleed much, but..."

But when you pull them apart, piece by piece, you're bound to find a little of the substance that created them.

Stefan grunted in acknowledgement as his gaze scanned the rest of the Watch. Grim faces and tight lips, one and all, eyed him with suppressed wariness. He'd reminded them why they called him Boss. He just wished he'd done it with a little more decorum.

"Have someone clean all this up. Don't mention any of this to Sasha," Stefan instructed. She wouldn't understand why Stefan had to keep her away.

"She know what happened?" Jameson asked quietly as they made their way over to Toa.

"Yes. I came clean."

"It help at all? With the nightmares?"

Jameson had lost a family member, too. Like Stefan, he blamed himself for not being there. They all did. They also blamed the *Mata* for fleeing like cowards.

Only Stefan lost a mother, though.

"She's not like...most females." Stefan cleared his throat. "She's...got my back."

Jameson gave a small nod. "Good. Helps to spread the wealth."

"Wealth, meaning, baggage?"

"Exactly. I plan to take the leadership when you make Regional. Just so you know."

Stefan bit back a laugh. That change in topic was welcomed. "I have to get through the Regional before I make Regional."

"Give Sasha a few hard knocks with the council, just to get her riled up, and you two will be unstoppable. She learns quickly, she's got limitless potential, and she's...got your back, like you said. It was the last boost you needed to step up."

"Chess board is set up, huh?" Stefan drolled as they neared a paler-than-usual Toa.

"She's not the only one that has your back. If that male was any whiter, he'd look like a snowman." Jameson smirked before peeling away toward the driver's side.

"Need to check out anything before we go?" Stefan asked Toa.

Toa just shook his head, for once with nothing to say. Stefan wished it would hold through the evening as well. They'd have to sit at the same dinner, after all. The same dinner, hoping no one had to challenge anyone else...

CHAPTER NINE

The women in the clearing sat with bowed heads, eyes closed, and breathing deeply. Focusing.

"Okay, women, call the corners," the leader said quietly. "Let's try to cleanse the negative feel of this place."

Dominicous and Jonas shifted at the same time, tiny movements hinting that their focus just got a lot more...focused.

The air electrified around us. Magic pulsed and beckoned, looming around me. Swirling and dancing, playful and joyous, it begged me to fill myself and become one with the women in the clearing. To suck in as much as I could hold and join hands. To laugh harder and louder than I ever had. A smile curled my face as Charles bent to regard my expression in confusion.

They can access their magic!

I felt the flame within each of them. The leader burned a bright orange, filled with a mass of raw, blasting power. The mousy one simmered with only green, but it twisted and churned in such a strange and intricate way. The twins each sported red, their faces screwed up in intense concentration.

"I thought you said humans couldn't access their magic." The words tumbled out of my gaping mouth quietly. They were like me! I could feel it. I could sense the *rightness* of it, the *sameness,* in a way I couldn't feel the clan's at all.

"What did you say?" Dominicous stepped close to me, bending to catch my words. "They have magic, did you say?"

"These old broads?" Charles whispered incredulously.

I opened up to the elements, feeling that rush as sweet magic filled my body. Without even thinking, I joined that throbbing elixir in the clearing. I entwined my magic within theirs, feeling the community of it in a way I'd never felt in my whole life. Feeling at one with it. I wasn't linked, because we weren't sharing power, but more...hanging around each other. Nodding to each other, magically.

"What is..." The leader's brow furrowed.

Almost immediately, that wrongness from the spell left behind sullied the magic. The jagged fragments corroded the natural world around it. A failed spell, maybe, but a nasty one.

The women were trying to wash away the magical stink. All they were succeeding at, however, was playing with the elements. They could suck in magic, but they weren't really doing anything with it. They lacked training and focus.

I didn't.

Without meaning to, I swept them all up into my focus, like holding hands from a distance; reveling in the unity, feeling the embrace of like-using magical people. Toa and I hadn't been able to do this—when my spell touched his magic, the power leaped to him, forcing a link. With these women, with similar magic, we just kind of kumbaya'ed around the clearing, beating our magical drums in harmony.

No, it wasn't strictly useful, magically speaking, but it was bolstering my spirits with each passing moment. *I wasn't alone!*

I analyzed the spell left behind. It hovered like a burned frame of a house, decrepit. Concentrating, trying not to laugh in glee, I smothered what was there while also knocking down the foundations. I wiped away solid traces of the spell, collapsing the rest of the framework with it.

"What's happening?" Charles asked. His hand squeezed my shoulder. "What are you doing with the magic?

I focused with all my being on one sticky part. Like an intricate knot in the hands of someone who bit their nails, I couldn't quite get it. I couldn't disentangle it. I could probably blow it up, which would greatly help my frustration, but it wouldn't help much else.

Just as I was about to throw up my hands and let it go, I felt a deft magical touch, as though soft, light hands covered mine and took over. With a complexity that would piss Toa off, the small details of the spell were finally unraveled. The rest of the magic disintegrated like snow falling, settling back into the world around it.

"What just happened?" Dominicous asked in a low hum. His gaze hit mine. "Did you unravel that spell?"

"What was that?" the leader asked, her eyes blinking open in confusion.

"Did you feel it?" the mousy woman asked, eyeing the leader.

I nodded at Dominicous dumbly, holding on to the feeling of this new magical community. Sisterhood. I wanted to hug somebody.

"Oh really? *Now* you want to get up on me? Woman, you're taken. Get off." Charles peeled my hands away with a grin.

"It worked!" one of the twins exclaimed in shock. "We did it." She paused, staring at the candles. "*How* did we do it? That was weird."

"But awesome," the other twin joined in.

They bobbed their heads in excitement and shared a high-five.

The leader and the mousy lady were staring, wide-eyed, at Dominicous. The leader's mouth dropped open.

And then things went pear-shaped.

"I'll get him!" the mousy lady squeaked.

She bounced up with a quickness that made Charles chuckle, although he did not react. Pepper spray held high, Taser coming up to join, she yelled, "Don't you come near us! Get out of here! We're not defenseless."

"There's another one over—" the leader's voice cut off in a moan.

"Don't you make them all lovey!" I screamed at Jonas while putting my hands up in surrender. "Don't you touch them, Jonas! You touch them and I will give you a seriously bad day."

"Night," Charles helped, a grin taking up his face as he watched the pepper spray draw near.

"What's happening?" one of the twins said, glancing around. "Oh whoa, those guys are huge. Look like a football team. How long have they been here?"

"I am strangely aroused," the leader said in a booming voice, her eyebrows in a flat line over her eyes. "I haven't been turned on in ten years. What kind of strange voodoo have we wandered into? Who are you? What do you want?"

"Get out of here!" Mousy growled at us, arsenal held up in thin, shaking arms. Her teeth bared in a human snarl.

"She's quite courageous," Dominicous noted. "I wonder how they are able to see through our magic cloak now when they couldn't a moment before."

"What are you staring at, young man?" The leader struggled to her feet, grass and mud clinging to her ample rear. She punched her fists to her hips in disappointment as she faced off to Jonas. "I'm not afraid of you, so you can quit that unbecoming scowl!"

This was getting out of control.

"I just worked magic with them somehow, I think. Or *around* them, anyway," I rattled off quickly to Dominicous as I stepped out, arms still raised to show I wasn't dangerous.

Seeing me, Mousy's expression waffled, confusion filtering in.

"Did you say you linked with them?" Dominicous asked in alarm, stepping forward with me, ready to shield my body from danger.

The finger on the pepper spray turned white. The arm started shaking violently. Not good.

"We are here for the same reasons you are," I said to Mousy in a calm, although slightly harried, voice. "We unraveled that spell together. I have the same magic you do. I can help you. You can help me. Maybe. Hopefully. At the minimum, we can just hang out and magically hold hands. I'd be into that."

"What's that?" The leader waved her hand in front of her face. It looked like she was trying to clear a bad smell. Her gaze shifted away from Jonas and over to us. "Good heavens—what are you doing out here at this hour? And with these men? This is no place for you, young lady."

"Well, we're here..." one of the twins mentioned.

"Can we all just sit down a minute and have a chat?" I asked slowly. "We'll just clear the air. I think that would be best."

The leader walked directly across the circle. My heart started thumping. She knew it had been "cleansed." That the nasty spell was dissolved away. She felt it.

My gaze slid to Dominicous. He winked. He'd noticed it, too.

"I'm Birdie." The larger woman gave a head bob. Apparently that was her version of shaking hands. Her notice flicked toward the mousy woman. "This is—would you put those down, Delilah?! Have you noticed the size of the men standing here? The Taser would probably tickle them."

"Nope," Charles muttered behind me.

"As I said, this is Delilah," Birdie went on. "She and I founded this circle about ten years ago. Three years ago, Jen and Liz joined up."

"The circle?" Dominicous asked pleasantly. "Can you talk about that, please?"

"Oh sure, but maybe we can move this chat away from here," Birdie said, looking around the area. Her gaze hit Jonas. A scowl creased her face. "The seclusion of this place attracts filth—keep frowning and your face will stay like that, you know."

"It's already locked on tight," I said, trying to hide my smile from Jonas. And failing.

Ann snickered somewhere behind us.

"Let's return to our vehicles, shall we?" Dominicous held his hand out to steer the group like any eighteenth-century gentleman would. "I am eager to return to the mansion. I think something pressing will need my attention."

With a shock of fear that Dominicous knew something I didn't, I focused on my link with Stefan. An undercurrent of sadness radiated. Sadness, and tinges of desperation. He was thinking of his parents—he only felt like this when the past reared its head and threatened to tear him down. Since the demon surfaced, he'd been struggling with this constantly. Something had triggered his memories, but overlaying that was determination and triumph. He was fighting through.

"I think you miss Toa more than he misses you," I joked with Dominicous as he escorted me out of the trees. "He was never all jumpy to get back to you when we were on the *Mata* property."

"I never get in over my head."

"What's Toa doing that he's in over his head? I'd love to witness that."

"I'm not sure," Dominicous answered quietly, "but whatever it is, it's made him feel inferior." His gaze hit mine as we stepped onto the pavement. "That's between us, of course. As family."

Warm fuzzies bubbled up my body. I shrugged with a shy smile. He turned to our followers, the group of women getting a better view of my crew as a streetlamp rained down light. Wide eyes there were in plenty.

Except for Birdie. She didn't seem fazed by much. "So what is this, then? Bodyguards?" Those fists found her hips again.

Jonas stepped away and pointed out towards the distant street. Charles did likewise, pointing back towards the park. Ann loitered near the Hummer, eyes always moving. You'd think we were in a combat zone instead of a deserted park.

"Did you feel a...presence back there?" I asked hesitantly. I didn't know how to come out and say, "Hey! You've got magic. So have I! Let's make a club!"

Birdie eyed me in speculation. It was Delilah that answered. "Was that you? We've always managed to call the corners successfully, but then...we just can't seem to direct our focus. We stalemate."

"*You* can't direct the focus, you mean," Birdie huffed. "*I* don't know how you do half of the things you manage."

"And what is it you manage?" Dominicous asked. "And these corners you speak of. That is...the elements? Magical forces?"

Delilah scrubbed at the ground with her toe. "We just mess around with our energies."

"Don't be bashful," Birdie interjected, stepping closer to her friend. "It is nothing to be embarrassed about." She faced off to Dominicous defensively. "We practice a form of Wicca

—a modern pagan, witchcraft religion. While we don't rip off our clothes in the moonlight and praise the Goddess and God, we do celebrate nature. We focus our energies and open up to the world around us. To the trees swaying, to the air displaced by a tiny insect, to the awe of watching the sunrise after a long night. We—"

"Are long-winded," Jonas growled. His plans for this night had been shot all to hell. Poor bugger.

Birdie didn't know the backstory, though. Her fisted arms rammed down at her sides. "This belief system goes back to the Paleolithic peoples, I'll have you know. To the cave paintings of the Hunter God and Fertility Goddess. It is old, passing through time and space—still around. And Witchcraft, something you might deem a silly little hobby idiot women get up to, is actually something known in ancient history as 'The Craft of the Wise' because most who followed the path were in tune with the forces of nature. Witches were anything from midwives to healers. We don't prance around, waving wands and sacrificing things to open fires. We are useful, damn it!"

"And do you practice tarot, perchance?" Dominicous asked softly.

One of the twins started fidgeting. Delilah lowered her head further as a shadow passed over Birdie's eyes. They thought they were beaten. They thought tarot proved their silliness. And they couldn't be more wrong. Not with this lot.

"Because I've been meaning to get my tarot read," I jumped in. "I've tried and I have no idea how."

"Me, too," Ann spoke up. She glanced at me, a sparkle in her eyes. "Seriously, I have. I tried to do it myself, but I have to read that stupid book that tells you what the cards mean. And there are different meanings when it's inverted, and..."

Charles glanced over at Ann. "You're a Shifter. Leave the magic to those who know what they're doing."

"I have magic, you dick. It just works differently than yours," she shot back.

"Can the preschoolers shut up for a second?" I rubbed my temples. I needed a more professional outfit. In defeat, I said, "Okay, I think we still have things to do tonight—"

"No," Jonas interrupted. "The Boss was called in to the other site. Toa has looked at it."

"Stefan...?" What I'd felt earlier swirled around me. "There was another demon? Stefan was called in without me?"

I looked down at the glowing face of my phone. Only one message: "Dinner will be fine. Dress up?"

"Why wouldn't he call? Wait—" I rounded on Jonas. "He was *supposed* to call. I was supposed to be contacted, right? As the mage of this territory?"

"Toa went in your stead. He qualifies," Dominicous countered mildly.

"That was my decision to make. Plus, Toa probably forced his way there. He doesn't trust Stefan not to freak out—" Another puzzle piece clicked into place. "He did freak out, didn't he? He tried to keep me away so he could go crazy."

"I think we need to first address the, very confused, young ladies in front of us. Then we can address the glitch in communication." Dominicous smiled down at the foursome.

I covered up the link. I didn't want Stefan to feel the anger headed his way. With a guy like him, you had to spring it on him, or you had no hope of it sticking.

"Yes, fine," I conceded. "That makes me mad, but okay."

"Just don't blow anything up," Charles droned.

I breathed in deep and squeezed my eyes shut for just one second. Regrouped, I put on a smile and addressed Birdie. "Sorry about all this. I'm still learning. Anyway, we have a different take on magic than you probably realize. For example..."

I sucked in the elements, mixing them just right. Barely thinking, I enclosed Charles in an extremely electric containment box. An extremely electric, *smallish* containment box. Mouth off again, I dare you.

Charles stood unnaturally still, glancing at the hazy black box around him.

"Throw something at him," I offered the women.

"Please don't," he muttered, not moving anything but his mouth and eyes.

"I will," Ann volunteered. She picked up a rock and threw it as hard as she could. A shower of sparks blasted out from point of contact, most of them on the outside of the box, but a few singeing his skin. He flinched, his eyebrows dipping low.

Jonas smirked.

"What is that..." Delilah leaned in, analyzing the box.

"Is this a trick of some kind?" Birdie asked.

I shook my head. "I'm human. Just like you. Magic is real. You felt me in your...circle earlier. Someone helped me with that spell. This is real, it's just not advertised."

"Then who are they?" Birdie motioned to the guys around me.

"That's a lesson for another day. For now, I want to get to know more about you. About your magic. See if you would be up for learning more about it. Maybe using it."

"Possibly you would like to come back to the mansion?" Dominicous asked.

"Just coerce them," Jonas grumbled. "Humans just need the suggestion and they fall in like sheep. Weak-willed race, all of them."

I'd had it.

Jonas was the next to get a black box. His glare made my butt tingle, but I didn't care. His tattoos swirled to life, orange and shimmering. With a hand like a claw, he raked down the front of the box. Sparks lit up the parking lot, burning his skin.

"What is he doing?" one of the twins exclaimed—they looked identical. I'd forgotten what name went with who.

"He's being cranky," I answered.

Jonas raked down again, trying to weaken the box with the runes swirling his arms. But I shot black. He'd try all night if he wanted. I may learn slow, but I did learn, so eat it.

I turned back to the girls as Charles said, "Just take it, bro. You don't want her to duel you. She comes up with nasty shit that hurts for a week. If you're lucky. One time, my balls literally itched for a month. No one wanted to touch me—thought I was the first to contract one of the human sexual viruses."

"This is quite entertaining, but it's getting late, Sasha," Dominicous chided gently. "I would like to check in with dinner preparations and speak with Toa."

"Yeah, sorry." I brushed my hair out of my face distractedly. "So, ladies, uh...do you want to learn more about your magic? Maybe come with us to the mansion—where we live? We can fill you in and maybe see about classes and whatnot."

"The mansion?" Birdie shook her head confusedly. "Listen, this is all...interesting, but Jen has a family to get back to, and the rest of us have to work tomorrow."

"Right, of course." I took out one of my newly printed business cards. Below my name was: "*Black*." Other than that, there was a phone number and address. That was it.

"Think about it. Think about how it felt when I joined your circle. About what I'm able to do with my magic. I know you could do that, too. You are able to access it, and that is the hardest part. Well, for most humans."

Birdie fingered the card before tucking it into a pocket in her skirt. "We'll see."

"And if you want," I continued, stepping toward the

retreating four girls, "come by tomorrow at sundown. Or any time tomorrow night."

Birdie gave me a small nod as she shepherded the girls away. I watched them walk away in silence, hoping beyond hope they chose to, at least, learn more. That feeling of unity, of harmony, had been so natural and gratifying. I wanted to feel it again; to work as a team. As a unit.

"They will come around," Dominicous said, moving toward the car. "They just have to allow time for their minds to expand and include these fantastic ideas. Human females are much better at adapting then males."

"Make them come around," Jonas growled, staring at me not unlike that caged demon the other day.

"I'm going to head out," Ann said, stepping closer. "I want to check in with Tim. Plus, I have a date."

"With whom?" Charles and I asked together.

Ann gave me a sly smile. "We'll chat later. Gotta run."

Without an ounce of bashfulness, she stripped down to nothing and handed me her clothes. "Keep those, would ya? Buying new clothes is getting expensive."

Green magic enveloped her, her grimace quickly changing into the furry face of a mountain lion. A feline purr echoed off the cars. With the grace only a big cat could muster, she turned tail and loped into the trees. Gone to hunt, or run, or just let her magical side run free. I smiled after her.

"Okay, let's get this show on the road." With a last glance toward the site that had held that nasty spell, I wondered, and feared at the same time, when another creation would be turned loose. And how powerful of a demon it would be.

CHAPTER TEN

"What the fuck is this?" Jonas roared, standing at the back of his Hummer.

I'd just spent a tense fifteen minutes sitting in confined quarters with Jonas and his simmering temper. Now we stood at the back of his car, seething rage turning into explosive language. Dominicous stepped back to see the problem, and then, grinning, wasn't helping.

Keeping my distance, I circled to the back of the car and found the issue. It was a bumper sticker that read, "Trust me, I'm hilarious."

Ann's doing, obviously.

"Everyone that knows you will know that thing is lying, bro," Charles helped, slinking away. "Sasha, I'm going to go eat. I've had about enough of you for one evening."

"Real nice," I muttered.

"I must get you to tell me a joke sometime," Dominicous said to Jonas.

"Okay, Jesus, you guys. You spend more time pestering each other than you do me, and that is saying something." I walked toward the mansion. Toward Stefan.

"Did you do this, human?" Jonas demanded, still standing at the back of the Hummer.

"No," I called.

"It was that mongrel. *Damn it!*"

"He is so easily riled up," Dominicous noted in his usual pleasantry, walking with me. Sometimes it was hard to remember he could rip someone's face off. And would, if the situation demanded it. "I wonder how he relieves his stress."

He didn't have long to wait to find out.

Jonas caught up to us as we entered the mansion. "Sasha, wait."

He stepped in front of me, his face red from willing calm. "In this territory, all things magical go through you. It is up to *you* to defer that authority to another. And while the Boss knows this, the most important thing to him is you. Your safety. He, more than most, will first act as your mate, and next as a leader. Some would say this is his greatest weakness, but in a race where procreation is hard, females that can bear children are, indeed, the most important, and therefore, no one will fault him too heavily.

"But as a co-leader, you need to balance his weaknesses, as he balances yours. If he steps on your position, it is up to *you* to set him right, aggressively if need be. The Boss has wronged you, and you need to see to it that he gets a hold of his shit, and doesn't do it again. We don't breed weak females, human. We don't breed females that will roll over and take what they are given. We are a warrior race. We fight for what's ours."

Jonas flexed, thick cords of terrifying muscle running from his head to his feet. His face went red. *This message will self-destruct in five, four...*

"I got it, Jonas. Go have sex. Mean, nasty, aggressive sex." I didn't dare pat him on the arm. You had to know when to leave the guy alone.

His crazy gaze slipped past the Regional as he turned. He strode down the hallway, flexed arms pushed away from his sides. A smaller guy stepped in front of him and loitered, apparently not having the presence of mind to look up. Big mistake.

With a roar, Jonas picked him up by the neck and the ass. Limbs on the guy flailing, mouth in a silent *oh*, Jonas hurled him through an open doorway. A thumping tumble indicated the guy had landed.

Jonas continued on his way as if nothing had happened.

"I can see why he doesn't get a multitude of challenges," Dominicous said, his expression pensive as he watched my helper stride away. "He is largely unpredictable and barely contained. He's had some emotional scarring, I think. He looks to Stefan, to his Boss, to keep him in line. To keep him grounded. That is wise, or else he would be a problem."

"Did you just see what he did? He threw some random guy through a doorway! He *is* a problem."

Dominicous turned his gaze back to me as we continued to the upper floors. "But he is on your side. More so than on Stefan's. He is rooting for you, or else why would he call his superior's personal motives down?"

"Well, he offered up his life to protect me. If I don't succeed, it will mean he made a bad decision. He doesn't say the words, 'I was wrong' all that often."

"Good. He is knowledgeable. I hope you don't mind if I keep an eye on him, though. I don't like such unpredictability so close to my daughter."

Dominicous deposited me in front of Stefan's and my wing. "Until dinner, then."

He offered a slight bow and continued on his way, his stride quickening without my shorter legs to hinder him.

What a weird night. And it wasn't over.

I paused outside the door as the familiar wave of longing

washed over me. Sometimes I hated this intense hunger to reconnect with him after even a short absence. It muddled my thoughts and got in the way of my agenda. Like right now, for example. I needed to be firm and steadfast, demanding what was mine and taking no compromise.

With a stern face and confident air, I steeled myself, then pushed through into the room. Plush and refined furnishings greeted me, welcoming me home. I found him in the living room area, sitting in front of a huge bay window, staring out at the night. His broad back faced me, the bump and divot of his muscles beckoning me closer.

Keep your head, Sasha. Don't let the prettiness distract you!

I cleared my throat. I would not request an audience, I would demand it.

He continued to stare out the window, completely lost in thought.

I cleared my throat again, louder this time.

Two onyx eyes flashed to my reflection in the window. He straightened up slowly, like a bear coming out of hibernation. His huge width of shoulder swiveled as he stood, higher and higher until he was standing over me from the other side of the room. Black slacks and a dress shirt perfectly outlined his stellar body. Freshly shaven and smelling like sin, the sight of him pushed all the air out of my lungs.

Jonas' growl sounded in my head, keeping my focus.

I raised my chin and prepared for a battle. "What's this I hear about you not contacting me with a demon sighting?"

"I needed to go without you. I needed to confront my past without fear you'd be affected."

Ah. Good explanation...

"You could have explained that, Stefan. It was my decision to make, not yours."

"Yes."

That earthshattering face stared at me, passive. Intense

love radiated through the link, infusing my body. His solid frame, filled with undeniable power and strength, seduced me closer. Increased my longing until I wanted nothing more than to fall in his arms.

"I need you to treat me like your mage," I pushed, desperately trying to ignore my body's treachery. "I'm not a trophy wife that might get hurt if I scratch my arm!"

"Scratching your arm would be getting hurt."

I gritted my teeth into his bemused, twinkling eyes. He wasn't taking this seriously. He hadn't been scared enough.

"When word comes in about something magical, that is *my* domain. I expect to be notified. Stefan, think of it from my point of view. I'm trying to fit into this place. There are certain codes you all live by, and I can't have you getting in my way when they involve me. Either you start acting like a leader, or I will start acting like you."

The twinkling in his eyes dulled. A small crease started between his eyebrows. "What does that mean? Start acting like me?"

"Do my own thing, and not involve you. My crew is loyal to me. The *Mata* are, too. If something comes up, like that demon the other day, I can simply...not let you know."

His fists clenched and unclenched. Muscles flexed and relaxed, straining his shirt. Remembering the fight earlier, or maybe from the demon the other day, had the link warring with rage, uncertainty, and, above all, possessiveness. He could not comprehend me facing that alone. Unprotected.

I stared into those liquid black eyes. The world fell away. Seeing him in that crisp white shirt, and the cufflinks, and designer slacks. He even had dress shoes on. The man looked like a million bucks wrapped in a deadly sin.

I tried to settle down, to simmer down my libido, but his predator was emerging, firing me up, getting my heart pumping. A burst of adrenaline attacked me, responding to his call to battle. Responding to what he would do if something ever happened to me. He slipped toward battle rage, and I slipped in as well. No battle to fight? No problem, we'd war with each other until climax.

I was striding at him before I knew what I was doing. He came at me just as fast. I ripped his shirt open, marveling at his perfect chest. I wrapped my hand around the back of his neck and pulled him toward me, capturing his mouth with mine. He ripped my pants away, undies discarded directly after that. He took down his pants right before I climbed onto his sizeable body, wrapping my legs around his waist, letting him take my weight. With a hard thrust, he pushed inside of me, filling me up.

His fist curled in my hair as his body pumped. I tightened my grip around his neck and scratched down his torso with my other hand. He growled in my ear before taking my earlobe in his teeth. I leaned against him suddenly, my shift in weight all on his shoulders. He staggered and lost his balance, toppling backwards.

We fell to the ground, me on top, striving harder. I rocked on top of him, taking all of him and pushing for more. Harder and harder we worked, clutching at each other, grimacing with the sweet pain of it. He yanked my hair. I dug my nails into his chest. Clenching his teeth, he grabbed my butt in two handfuls and crashed my body down on top of his. I used my weight to help, pounding.

"Al-most there," I groaned.

He yanked my hair again, my scalp protesting, my sexy systems feeding off of the aggressive lovemaking.

"Harder!" I yelled, my eyes fluttering.

He turned over suddenly, pulling me beneath him. Large hands on the backs of my knees, he forced my legs over his shoulders. His manhood dove into my sex like a raging warrior, oh-so-deep, hitting new places with fervor. Losing my breath, everything started to condense. Pain budding, and then flowering pleasure, riddled my body. His hip joints rammed into my smooth thighs. His hard manhood plunged into my soft depths.

"Oh god, oh god," I repeated over and over. Clutching harder. Hanging on for dear life now. Almost … .

"OH!" I exalted. The orgasm was so intense, it probably looked like I was being electrocuted. "*Wow*!"

Stefan, breathing heavy, braced his hands on either side of me. Eyes connected with mine, he said, "Fine. I will keep you in the loop. But if I hear of you rushing into danger without me, I will not be so easily yielding."

"Easily yielding? You? Yeah, and Jonas sings songs in flower-filled fields. Give over."

A grin worked up Stefan's face. "Huh?"

"Never mind. Let me up. I have to shower and change. We'll be late."

"I *was* ready," Stefan said, pulling me up with him. "But then you accosted me. I think Jonas' temper is rubbing off on you."

"Do what I say and we wouldn't have this problem."

"I do what you say. Afterwards."

I huffed, the small kinks in my neck loosening. "Oh, and I think I found some witches that actually know how to use their magic. Far out, right?"

"Far out?"

"Hippy slang." I proceeded to tell him about the four-pack of women. So unexpected, but hopefully, a great find. They just needed to learn to use their magic.

No biggie.

CHAPTER ELEVEN

Dominicous pushed open the door slowly, wondering what kind of mood he'd find his mage in. The blood link was filled with icy determination, which was like a blind. Really anything could be kicking around the analytical and insightful blond head.

A quiet walk through the meeting area of the large guest suite revealed no Toa. Dominicous continued to the dining area, and then the book room. Nothing. Finally, he poked his head in the mage's bedroom.

Blond head bowed over his clasped fingers, Toa sat on the edge of his bed, naked, eyes closed.

"Everything...okay?" Dominicous ventured.

"I've sexed my way through this house. It hasn't taken my mind off of the crossroads we've landed in."

Dominicous stepped in slowly, keeping to the wall. "Oh?"

"Your chosen daughter will mate that...male. He will be tied to us. I do not know if this was a stroke of luck, or the ruiner of our lives."

"Come now, Toa. That's a little on the dramatic side. "

Even for you. "He's young. He's had some trauma in his youth that he is working through. Whatever happened today—"

The desperation on Toa's face as he lifted his head cut Dominicous off. "Whatever *happened* today..."

The words lingered. Floating through the silent room. Bloodshot blue eyes held Dominicous. "He single-handedly took out a lower-level demon. I've heard that he can take out up to three *Dulcha*, all on his own. His speed, his power—he would beat you in a fight, Dominicous. I saw proof of that today. What's more, with Sasha standing behind him, bracing him against his fears, his potential is limitless. *Limitless,* Dominicous."

"But, as you said, he is tied to us." Dominicous couldn't help the edge to his voice. He didn't like being told he had shortcomings, even if it was just a product of Toa's dramatic nature. Sometimes he wished Toa would only show him the refined, subtle side he showed everyone else. It'd be so much less tedious in these situations.

"Do you not see the long-term implications, Dominicous? She is black, he is burnished gold, rising into the white with her blood. They each have special abilities that work best together. They are kismet, somehow. Made for each other. Fate has attached a chain to them, and we've grabbed on and are now being dragged behind them into a snake pit. We will be pushed aside so the council members, or whoever else, can get their hands on special talent."

"But one is human. Surely she won't be as coveted."

"Oh, bah!" Toa batted the air. "Once we can link with her, she will always be coveted—she is black. And she doesn't blink an eye at our culture."

Dominicous wasn't so sure about that, but he sidestepped that landmine for now. "Well, then, it is a great thing she is my daughter, her future mate is this wonder warrior, and we are all going to the council meeting together. Rising in the ranks was always my plan, as you know, and now I have someone to govern my back. Someone willing and able. I think this, in fact, is the greatest news. You see, all you needed was a small dose of reality and a great many orgasms."

"What happens when he wants your mantle?" Toa accused, standing.

"You forget," Dominicous' voice dropped an octave, "he doesn't have the political know-how I do. He is young. He's done well with this clan, but stepping up into Regional will be a giant adjustment."

"And what if you don't have anywhere to step up into? Then what happens?"

Dominicous leveled him with a glare, cutting down the excessive dramatics. "I think we will operate with the assumption that he being tied to us is a stroke of luck. I saved Fate's vehicle. She was then given a mighty alpha with, as you say, limitless potential. Only after this was she returned to me. A collection of people, who previously had no family, are now merging together, starting with this dinner. That leg of the circle is complete. A new chapter begins."

"A new chapter of war. Of lies and deceit and probably the destruction of our customs."

Dominicous wanted to find a quiet corner and rub his temples in peace. Between the strange, though intensely humorous, personalities gathered around Sasha, and the threat of these demons, he wasn't sure he had enough patience to handle Toa's severe mood swings. Ever since they'd discovered Sasha was black, and also the little girl they saved, Toa had been on a Doomsday parade—planned, hosted and marched all by himself.

"Actually," Dominicous said, walking out of the bedroom and settling on the couch. Toa didn't follow.

"Actually," he started again, "there is an interesting—"

"*What?*" Toa demanded from the doorway. "You know I hate when you wander off while you are speaking to me."

"There is an interesting twist on today's routine outing. We found some witches."

Toa drifted in, his anxiety quickly being tucked back into wherever he stored it when his intellect was fired up. "Witches?"

"Yes. Apparently they cannot only access the elements, but Sasha noted that she found unity with them. That she joined with them, in some way. I don't think it was an established link, but from what it seemed, it wasn't far from."

Toa sat down slowly, riveted. "Explain."

Dominicous went over their encounter, re-explaining some nuances only Toa would find intriguing. When he was finished, Toa had yet to blink.

"What do you think?" Dominicous asked.

"She said she felt unity? That was the word she used?"

Dominicous tilted his head yes.

Toa sat back slowly and clasped his hands. "There was much talk in the old era of covens and unity. A form of sisterhood. Within these circles, as they called them, the women grew and expanded, creating a circular form of hierarchy greatly different to that of men. A matriarch would steer their united minds, much like within elephant culture. Within this protective horde, they would bind together, the strong helping the weak by bringing them into a collective whole."

"Synergy," Dominicous said, finally rubbing his temples. Mood swings and now lectures. He didn't know how Sasha did it. Toa would not sit comfortably until he had all the riddles in his environment solved, and with Sasha, there were more riddles than solutions.

"Synergy, yes. Comes from the Greek word *synergia*.

Meaning working together. In modern times it simply means the whole is greater than the sum of its parts. Corporations use this ideology within their vertical integration."

Dominicous exhaled slowly, rubbing faster.

"I am encouraged that Sasha was able to join this magical myth," Toa reflected.

"Maybe it's not a myth."

"Oh, I have no doubt. I just hadn't seen the theory in practice. I am intrigued and hopeful at the same time. This could be a helping hand—a team for Sasha to grow within. Tell me, did they have any control over their magic?"

"I think they could just call the elements. But Sasha did say one of them helped her unravel a tough spot in the spell."

Toa leaned forward, his attention unwavering. "Fascinating. I wish to meet them. Did you bring them back?"

"No. Sasha travels with a group of people that keep her grounded. Their unique bond works because it isn't confined to the strict and disciplined hierarchy Stefan has created—"

Toa waved away the words like he might a swarm of mosquitos. "I know who guards her. They show their love through their humor or malice. What is the point?"

"Her troupe isn't conducive to a first greeting. The witches were intrigued but hesitant. One has children, I understand."

"Didn't they just *dose* them and haul them back?"

Dominicous took his fingers from his temples. "Sasha is not from our people. She has more regard for humans than...many do."

"Pity—oh, don't go choosing *this* topic to suddenly get serious about. I agree, we need to change our philosophies with regards to humans if we ever expect to live cohesively, yes. But let's not forget, we've been hunted, tortured, and burned at the stake by their hand. You still have the scars to show it, I might remind you. Suddenly making way for an inferior species, a species that is capable of more violence than we have shown at the worst of times—capable of that violence to *each other* no less—is a tough pill to choke down."

"Humans, as a mass, can be small-minded, yes, showing extreme aggression when afraid. But wouldn't it be just as small-minded to show the same attributes? Wouldn't you rather rise above their simpleton fears and embrace what they have to offer instead? On an individual level, humans are capable of great understanding. Shouldn't we be, then, too?"

Toa leveled a placating look at Dominicous. "Can we have this debate another time? I don't have the energy."

"Of course," Dominicous conceded, bowing his head slightly. "And when we have that debate, I will mention that interacting more with humans, without the use of pheromones, will help us find groups of women like these witches. It was a sort of social club. One or two do tarot—maybe they have the gift of sight. There are bound to be more. I would like to speak with Stefan and Sasha about where to possibly look. And there is the child to think of. Or children, hopefully."

"Do you suspect these witches you found will seek us out? They can see us—Sasha's influence must have opened their eyes."

"Or possibly, actually *working* with the elements helped them expand their mind to take in more of their surroundings. All humans can see us if they really *look.*"

"True." Toa sat in repose for a moment, pondering. He rose slowly. "If these witches worked with Sasha as you say, then I might be able to work in a backdoor to link with her."

"If I were you, I would let Stefan facilitate that link. He seems to connect with her easily—to balance out her flow."

"I don't trust him."

"Being afraid is different than not trusting."

Toa's icy blue eyes shocked into Dominicous. "I am afraid

because I don't trust him. He is capable of great violence while being haunted by extreme emotional demons. That is not a great combination."

"Do you not remember me when you first met me?"

"I was afraid of you, also."

CHAPTER TWELVE

I stepped out of the bathroom amid a cloud of hairspray. I strolled by the full-length mirror to check out my wares. Sparkly midnight blue dress, *check*. A lacy and intricate necklace draping down my cleavage in a shimmer of diamonds, *check*. Dull brown hair coated with a ton of product for a high gloss, *check*.

Yup, I was rockin' it!

I ran my fingers along the exquisite, though probably extremely expensive, diamond necklace. Stefan had laid it on my pillow one night, asking me to wear his collar. Obviously I punched him, which he thought hilarious, but the sentiment brought tears to my eyes. It was beautiful, and what's more, it wasn't given because of an occasion. It wasn't my birthday or Christmas—it wasn't even Valentine's Day—he'd just wanted to show his regard for me. He wanted to remind me that his job was to make sure I had everything I could possibly want. It was his way of providing for me.

This species was brutal, violent, and barbaric at times, but man-oh-man did they know how to treat a woman. Once you went *homo sacturine*, you never went back.

I paused for a moment. I was pretty sure that was their scientific name. But it was tucked into one of Toa's long-winded explanations, so I really couldn't be sure. People, but not humans. Male, but not man. Douche, and completely ridiculous at times.

Although, *homo* meant human, so technically, they were human. Don't tell them that, though. They'll then lecture you on how human scientists noticed the differences in the few specimens they found, but had no answers to define those differences. At least, not before they lost their memory. And their research.

I shook my head and headed out to the living room. If I wasn't careful, Toa's voice would be on a lecture loop inside my head—that's how much I heard him speak.

As I stepped into the living room I caught movement on the couch. I smiled in greeting, only to see the world's ugliest crocheted quilt in the making.

"What are you doing here?" I asked Charles. "And why can't you choose some decent colors for once?"

Charles' eyebrows crawled up his forehead. "This is for a little girl. So these colors work. Little girls like green and pink, you said so yourself. And I am sitting here because the Boss wanted to check in with Jameson about the various patrols. Everyone is expecting another demon sighting—the Boss just wants to make sure the patrols keep their eyes open and know what to look for."

"Uh, huh. Except, that is puke greenish-yellow, and fluorescent orange-pink. *No one* would want those colors, Charles. Boy, girl, your people, mine—no one. A dog maybe. Maybe a dog wouldn't mind."

"Well, then," Charles answered, unperturbed. "I've changed my mind. I am making this for a little dog. There. Happy?"

"Do you know anyone that has a dog?"

"The same number of people that I know of who have a little girl."

I grinned. "Let me guess—"

"None. Exactly," Charles cut me off. "My genius can't just sit around and wait for someone to request a quilt."

"Oh, *gen*ius. Is that what you're calling it? I can think of a couple other words."

"Insightful, handsome, great with his tongue..."

I tapped my chin in mock thought. "Nope. None of those."

"How would you know? You never let me show you how thoroughly I dip the wick."

"I have someone better for that. Right? Didn't you say you couldn't handle Darla? And that you had no idea how Stefan did?"

Charles gave me a pronounced shiver. "I just lost interest in this conversation."

"Didn't you wonder how the Boss could go without ever—"

"I said I was done."

"—giving blood? How he could keep—"

"Seriously, Sasha, she was a black spot on my record."

"—her in her place? *Beneath* him?"

Charles stood up and tucked his project under his arm. "Foul play. That was below the belt."

Chin high, Charles strolled out of the room, stray pieces of yarn dangling behind him. I couldn't help but snicker—score a point for me. Although, now I had no one to talk to.

As I was making my way to the window, the sky lightening with the approaching dawn, the door opened for the second time. Half expecting Jonas, because I always seemed to have one or other hanging around, I threw a glance behind me. And stopped dead.

Stefan stood in the doorway, broad shoulders nearly

touching the door jam on each side. He wore a perfectly tailored suit that molded to his body in a sleek and delicious way. Forget a dress shirt, the jacket looked so much more heavenly.

"Hi," I breathed, that constant tingling niggling at my core again. The man could turn me on by just showing up.

"You have our link blocked. Why?" he asked in that masculine growl, scouring me with his gaze. "Gods, Sasha, you look beautiful. The best of your species."

I gushed and strolled toward him, really trying for sexy. I opened the link, feeling desire and the underlying love radiating between us. "I was experimenting with my link to Dominicous. My...uh, father. Kinda."

A soft smile graced Stefan's handsome face. He let the back of his fingertips trail down my skin. "He is your father now. Enjoy it. Relish it."

A small tinge of sadness swirled in the link. I brought him closer for a kiss. "He'll be your father-in-law. We'll be one big, happy family. Me, you, Dominicous, and Sir Stares-A-Lot."

A bark of laughter rumbled out of his chest. "Can't wait. Shall we?"

"Who does Jonas get to go to town on?" I asked as we stepped out into the hall.

Charles flashed me a glare before calming his features for Stefan. "Do you need me anymore, Boss? Can you handle her?"

"Better than you can, yes. You can go."

"Oh, well, everyone's a critic today," Charles mumbled as he took himself the opposite direction down the hall.

"Go to town on?" Stefan asked softly.

"Yeah. I wouldn't want to be on the receiving end of a big, leather paddle. Doesn't he practice BDSM and what not? To relieve his temper?"

"Ah." Stefan nodded to a fierce-eyed woman passing us in the hall.

"Boss. Mage." The woman touched her heart.

"Sandra, right? She's in the Watch?" I recalled.

"Estel. She's in charge of the grounds. Great magic worker—terrible with a sword."

Damn it! There were so many people, all of whom were brand new to me. It was taking a long time to get everyone's name, not to mention their duties as well.

"Anyway," Stefan went on. "He only engages in that type of sex when he's on the receiving end. You have to be in firm control when you're the one in charge. Since he only reaches for that vice when he's *not* in control, he challenges people to attempt to dominate him. One female can do it repeatedly, and isn't afraid to."

I realized belatedly that my mouth was hanging open. "He's ... the one getting whipped and all that? By a chick?"

"Yes. It can be quite erotic."

"Have you done it?"

Stefan gave me a perplexed glance. "Of course. I don't much like it, though. If it's to be rough, I prefer war. All parties fighting to get closer. But if you wanted to try..."

"Nope." I stared straight ahead. "I'm good. War is good. I have no desire to whip you. Or get whipped—I'd probably lose my gravity and think someone is accosting me."

"Someone would be accosting you."

"And then I would reach for magic and accost him back..."

"Not if I did it right..." Stefan countered softly.

I couldn't help the giggle.

We paused in front of Dominicous' door. Stefan took a steadying breath as I said, "Speaking of dominance games... we're not playing them in here tonight. We're just getting to know our new family. That's all."

Stefan nodded. "Easier said than done."

"I know."

A knock brought Dominicous to the door. He gave me a small smile, and then bowed to Stefan. "Welcome. Please, come in."

We stepped into the same finery that the whole mansion had, with the same classy yet conservative furnishings and décor. Stefan had a quick glance around, surveying, before he honed back in on Dominicous, who was waiting by the couch.

"I trust everything remains to your satisfaction?" Stefan said in firm tones.

"Everything is perfect. Please, come in. Sit down. We've left our titles outside. In here, tonight, we are two different species having a quiet evening."

With a small tug on Stefan's hand, I led the way to the couch and sank in. Stefan leaned back and draped his arm over the back behind me. Dominicous sat in a recliner as Toa emerged from one of the bedrooms. He wore a strange Kimono-style robe with his feather-blond hair draping around his face.

Odd.

"Welcome, Sasha. Stefan." Toa brought over a tray with glasses of red wine. "We have no servants tonight. No helpers. Just us. Easy and friendly."

I blinked a couple times as I took my glass. It wasn't the most comfortable start to a comfortable evening.

After another glass of wine and some random small talk about the weather and Stefan's operations, a small knock sounded at the door. Toa glided over immediately, coming back with a wheeled tray covered in silver domes.

"No servants, I thought," I commented lightly as I got up to help load the trays onto the table. "Are these all the same?"

"Sasha, I am fascinated with these witches you found," Toa responded, straightening next to me.

"Oh. Yes. Um...but these dishes—are they all the same?"

"Yes, of course. Burgers or some such. Dominicous is pandering to you. He kept with your choice of cuisine. I have no idea why."

I squinted my eyes into his blue stare. "When you choose something, you like it better when someone ignores you and gives you something else?"

Toa cocked his head to the side. "Hamburgers, Sasha? I would not choose hamburgers. They are for barbarian Americans. I pushed for a beautiful rack of lamb with a wine reduction demiglaze and a touch of mint sauce."

"Toa, you're making me tired. C'mon you guys, come eat," I called.

"She doesn't like when we dally to the table," Stefan informed Dominicous with twinkling eyes.

Being that he was starting to relax, and also that it was true and justifiable, I ignored him. I also ignored the pat on the butt. I sat in the chair he pulled out for me, and waited while Stefan whisked the silver dome off my plate.

After I had sat, everyone around me sat as well, gentlemen of old. Only Toa stared down at his giant, half-pound burger in distaste.

"So, Stefan, what's next for you?" Dominicous asked as he took a huge bite of his burger.

"I assume you mean, when do I plan to seek elevation to your position?" Stefan took his own giant bite.

"Um, hum," Dominicous mumbled through a full mouth. Along with titles, the guys were also shedding their table manners. Give them an inch...

"Savages," Toa breathed.

"You might have noticed my...current problem with groveling," Stefan said lightly, wiping his face and taking a sip of wine.

Dominicous nodded, his gaze hitting mine across the table. "I have. I plan to move up as well. I wanted to caution you, however." His focus went back to Stefan, seriousness seeping into the previously calm air around them. "The higher up you climb, the more political the arena gets. It's no longer about intelligence, business, magic and brawn. There is a fifth element. And with an ace in the hole—" I got a flick of the eyes "—you won't have an easy time of it."

"Without help," Toa added. "It would be folly to lose your head and challenge Dominicous before it's time. This is a game. A strategy."

Stefan eyed the men with a firm mask. The link warred with wariness, spicy determination, and hope. It was the latter which gave me pause.

"I am your asset, Stefan," Dominicous said evenly, burger forgotten. "I will pave the way."

"And what do you get?" Stefan shot back.

"There is a saying in American football—protect the blind side. When I go into the hornet's nest, I want someone I can trust behind me, cutting off the rear attack. Working together, we can grant our own destiny. Alone, and we will each work harder. Had I not found Toa early, I would've been ripped apart and stashed away as a guard. Or a forgotten warrior."

"But, wouldn't they want to use your talents? Why would they want to get rid of you?" I asked.

Toa opened his mouth to reply, but Dominicous beat him to it. "The council needs strength and smarts, but they are old. They've been in power too long. They refuse to notice the world changing around them. It is why a faction of our kind are trying to push their way to the forefront of human society. It is why people like Trek have been allowed to cause so much havoc. A new bright star comes through, and the minions of these old, decrepit men get worried. They fear they'll lose their position. So they do what any brutal, corrupt society would do: get rid of the competition."

Dominicous stared at Stefan. Stefan stared back. The link colored with uncertainty. Stefan's gaze shifted to mine slowly. "I'll be fine. With Jonas and Jameson at my back, I'm covered."

"Maybe," Dominicous said slowly. "But without this clan at Sasha's back, she is exposed. Jameson, I believe, did not alert her to the demon earlier. You instructed him not to. And he left it at that. He is *your* man, not this clan's man, or he would have followed protocol."

Stefan tensed. But, just as quickly, eased back down. He leaned back. "I'm in a difficult position. I've marked her, so I have those obligations, but..."

"I understand." Dominicous nodded. "I am also in a difficult position. Family first. Survival of the species above all else. It doesn't help, of course, that she's human. It will take longer for her to gain support. But not to fear; we have Toa to think of all the possible strategies associated with this predicament."

Toa, just about to say something, closed his mouth with a snap. His focus shifted sideways to Dominicous. "I wasn't aware you planned to let on that you lack a sense of humor."

Oh my god! I couldn't help a delighted grin. Dominicous made fun of Toa! How had he not mentioned they had this relationship?

Stefan reached under the table and put his hand on my knee, the link filtering his delight even though his face didn't show it. He thought it was hilarious, too!

"Sasha, are you not planning to finish your burger?" Dominicous asked with a twinkle in his eyes. "I ordered it specifically for you. Bacon and all."

"I know. Toa already filled me on my barbaric tastes..."

"Yes, of course, let's make me the focal point of the tomfoolery." Toa took a drink of his wine in distaste as everyone else stifled their laughter.

After dinner we moved back to the living room. I was absolutely delighted to learn how relaxed and good-natured Dominicous was. Also, what a tight-knit bond he had with Toa, even though they were complete opposites. They worked off each other well, one always having the answers if the other didn't. And then, after a couple glasses of wine too many—I didn't have nearly the mass that these guys did—I asked it. I couldn't help myself.

"So, are you guys, like, a couple? 'Cause I had thought you were, but you don't really act like it the more I get to know you, so..."

"The closeness of our relationship comes from extensive battles," Dominicous answered. "You develop a tight bond with someone you have fought beside and thought you'd die beside. For example, you have a close relationship with Charles born of close calls and loyalty. You are also now forming a relationship with Jonas."

I eyed Stefan. He was staring back at me. "Not sexual," I clarified, raising my hands in surrender. "I don't like whipping people. Probably."

"We prefer the opposite sex, when we are given the choice," Toa explained patiently. "We don't have the set rules and criteria humans do in this age. Humans didn't used to be so rigid, of course. Back in the—"

"Forget I asked!" I said quickly. "Never mind. You dig sex. I get it."

Toa blinked twice and allowed himself to be distracted as he said, "But I do find the animal costumes strange. Stefan, I hope your people don't practice—"

"Don't even go there," I cut him off again. "I asked that question once. No animals."

When I had asked, Charles looked at me like I'd grown a third eye and also lost the use of my brain. Which was good, obviously, but still—it's not like it was a far-out question.

'I think it's time for bed," I said. "I get a day off tomorrow, and I'm going to take it."

Dominicous nodded and stood. He wrapped me in a big hug, his smell strangely familiar. Like a blankie, long forgotten. It was then I felt it. A warmth resonating deep, deep within me. Past all the cobwebs and under a bunch of rubble, I could feel a pulsing warmth of enchantment coming from him.

The enchantment of a parent with an offspring. His feelings for me, much stronger than before.

He backed off, surprised. His gaze flicked up to Stefan before he stepped back entirely. "I enjoyed spending this dawning with you, Sasha, and the night before it. I am sorry I didn't take you with me that night, so long ago. I should have. I knew your family had died. I thought humans could take better care of their own. It seems I was wrong."

My eyes started to sting. Stefan's arm came around me. I said, "You saved my life. And I became me. And then ended up in the same spot. So I think it worked out all right."

Dominicous smiled.

As Stefan and I made our way to our wing, Stefan said, "What shocked you? What happened?"

"I could kinda feel his emotions. More than before."

"He's your father, that might come in handy some time." After a pause he said, "I enjoyed myself tonight. He and I ... we have a lot in common. A lot of common ground. Under normal circumstances, we wouldn't be able to speak so openly about it."

"A night for many surprises."

I got a squeeze. "Let's just hope the surprises end with personalities behind closed doors."

That would be nice. Somehow I doubted it, though.

CHAPTER THIRTEEN

Charles' cell phone let off a shrill cry. Bleary eyed and sore-balled, Charles patted the nightstand. Squinting into the glare of its face, he tapped the answer button.

"What?"

"Charles? This is Rickie."

"Yeah. I can read. What do you want? It's the middle of the day."

"Who's supposed to be guarding Sasha today?"

"The Boss. You know, that crazy fucking male she's nearly mated to? The one she sleeps with. The one that *has his own phone line!*"

"Right. Except, she's got some visitors."

Wanting to cry like a little bitch—Charles hated being woken up in the middle of a sleep cycle—he rubbed his face and sat up. His balls protested immediately. He should've stopped Jasmine from her kung fu grip. And if her mouth wasn't working wonders on his cock, he would've.

"Charles?"

"Great gods, *what?* Give a male a chance to get his

thoughts in line, would ya? Who is it? Because if it's a demon, I'm not the person to activate the phone tree."

"A bunch of human women," Rickie answered with a shaking voice. "One of them is pretty pushy. Has the mage's card and everything. Demanding to see her. And ... they can see me. And this whole house..."

After a silent beat, in which Charles sat with his face in his palm, Rickie squeaked, "Did I mention that they're human?"

Charles groaned and fell back into the bed. "*Night!* She told them to come around at *night!*"

"Excuse me, sir?"

"Call Jonas. It's his turn."

"Yes, si—"

Charles hung up and stuffed the pillow over his face, shutting his eyes tight and letting his mind drift into the first stages of sleep.

His snooze was interrupted by a loud *crash*.

Charles rocketed out of bed before he knew what was happening. The door slammed against the wall, rebounding back into Jonas' outstretched hand. Jonas stood in the doorway naked, scratches and lacerations all down his front, some oozing red streaks. The doorframe lay splintered and devastated.

"What the hell, Jonas?" Charles yelled.

"My body is on fire," Jonas growled. "Get your dumb ass up and go let those old crones in. They have magic. Sasha's form of magic. We need them."

"You go get them," Charles snarled back. "My balls feel like someone is yanking on 'em. I just got to sleep."

"The day you can take a beating from a paddle with spikes in it, is the day I'll give a shit. You're first watch. I need to shower blood off, and then I'll join you. *Go!*"

For the first time in his life, Charles really wanted to go

head-to-head with this headstrong jackass. He was sick of this bullheaded song and dance, and Charles was pretty sure he could hold his own and even the balance of dominance. Unfortunately, his balls did really hurt, and Jonas had a point.

"Screw it." Charles snatched up some clothes and shoved past his prickly counterpart. He stalked through the mostly quiet hallways, daring anyone to ask him a question. He stomped down a couple steps before the throbbing in his crotch slowed him, and then made the rest of the way down gingerly. He really needed to start picking who he had sex with. There were plenty of females that *didn't* get off on a man yelping.

The women stood in the front entryway, staring down an extremely uncertain Rickie. Birdie stood at the front, checking things out like an army captain surveying a battlefield. The others were there, too, waiting behind her like skittish baby horses.

"Ladies, I thought Sasha told you to come in the *evening?*" Charles asked as he sauntered up, squinting in the glare of the many windows.

The leader put her fists on her hips. "Where did this house come from? I have lived in this city all my life, and I have never seen this monstrosity out here on the outskirts."

Charles rubbed his face. "You aren't as susceptible to concealing spells anymore because you have a better grasp on your magic. It's a weak spell, aimed mostly for humans. Hence, you are now seeing something that has been here all your life."

"Hmph." She looked around, eyeing Rickie, who was standing guard in a terrified sort of way. "So this is real, then. All this. What we've been doing. Why are you only now making contact?"

"That'd be Sasha. Our human. We don't usually mess

around with your kind. You're prone to pushing red buttons that kill a lot of people."

Her bushy eyebrows lowered over her eyes. "*Your* human? What is that supposed to mean? And just who do you think—"

She cut off as Jonas entered the room. All the nasty cuts and scrapes from his forays were hidden discreetly beneath a black turtleneck and equally black slacks.

"Look, ladies," Charles said. "Why don't you go and—"

"Come with us," Jonas interrupted. His patient and relaxed gaze turned to Charles. "Lead the ladies up to the Purple Room. I'll grab the mages and meet you there."

"In the middle of the day? Sasha was drinking at dawn. She's not going to be much good."

A shadow passed over Jonas' eyes, giving Charles a momentary thrill.

"I think you should let the mages make that decision," Jonas said in a low voice.

Charles didn't bother stifling the groan. "Okay, ladies, let's go. We're off to see the wizard. Although, she's not going to be so wonderful at this time of day."

As they passed through the adjacent room, aiming for the hallway so they could go up a level to the large and formal Purple Room, he heard gasps behind him. All four women had stopped midway through a lounge and were staring at a youngish male sitting on a couch naked, stroking his dick.

"Young man!" Birdie hollered. "Just what do you think you're doing with that thing? And why are you sitting in a communal area without a stitch? You march right up to your room this instant and put something on! And leave that thing alone—you'll go blind!"

The male's mouth dropped open. His bewildered gaze hit Charles, unsure what was happening and if he should follow this strange human's command.

"What are you doing up so late?" Charles asked, a grin working up his face.

"Cramming for a test. Just taking a break." His hand slowly left his erection.

"Oh my god…" Delilah breathed, her wide eyes glued to his naked body. Her face went deep crimson as her hand drifted up to cover her mouth.

"Stop gawking, women!" Birdie demanded. Her accusing glare hit Charles. "What is going on here? What have you led us into?"

"Nice body, though," one of the twins noticed quietly.

"Alright, come on." Charles motioned them on. "You can talk to Sasha about our culture. Just be thankful you came when no one was around. We like to keep our downtime physical."

"This was a bad idea," Birdie muttered, slowing them down so she could peer into all the rooms she passed and squinting into crevices just in case other naked men lurked.

They filed into the Purple Room not much later, shortly thereafter joined by a fuzzy-faced Sasha. Her bleary gaze took in the women as she sank into a couch in the middle of the room. "Hi. Sorry for my appearance—we kind of operate in the nighttime here. Everyone is mostly asleep in the day."

"Do you know what I saw on the way—" Birdie cut off as Toa's perfectly quaffed blond head entered the room. The male looked like he'd had a full night's sleep, a hairdresser, and a facial.

How did he do it?

Jonas walked in behind them, peeling away to the side and standing by the far wall.

"Hello," Toa said, touching each of them with his gaze. "I hear you practice the art of Wicca. How extraordinary. I hope you don't mind me assessing you, since you were gracious enough to show up today."

The twins smiled, letting him direct them to take a seat. Delilah turned red again and followed suit.

"Fantastic," Toa said as he sat gracefully next to Sasha. "Now, I wondered if you might call the..." Toa raised his eyebrows in silent question.

"Corners," Birdie helped, preferring to stay standing. Probably wanted to scout out the shadows in the room to make sure there were no naked men hiding.

"Yes, of course. Please," Toa gestured her toward a seat, "at your leisure."

"He kind of looks like a vampire," one of the twins muttered to the other, her smile taking up her whole face. "Like one of the cast members in *Twilight*."

"He's definitely hotter than Edward," the other answered, giggling.

"Ladies," Birdie admonished, finally settling directly onto the carpet in the middle of the room. "Join the circle and let's call the corners."

"Can I sit with you?" Sasha asked shyly.

"Of course, dear, come over. And your friend, too, if he likes."

"I can observe from here," Toa answered with a respectful nod. "Please, just go about your normal routine."

The women settled in their circle, heads bowed and eyes closed. Except Sasha, who was looking around at the others, probably trying to feel what they were doing. After a few sighs, and some deep breathing, suddenly Sasha's tired and haggard face bloomed with a smile. She closed her eyes in contentment.

"Unity, yes," Toa noted, leaning forward in his seat.

Charles could feel the fan of Sasha, urging his magic higher. Urging him to fill his body and pull in just a little bit more. He let it, and then sat forward with Toa.

Electricity filled the air, calling to his magic, swirling

around him. He connected with it, feeling a floral essence, as if rose petals fell softly across his body.

"That's so neat," Delilah said, her eyes opening and going right to him. "Is that you? Can you do this, too? It seems male."

"You have linked with me, actually," Toa said calmly. "It is not male. Magic is not relegated to sex. It is two poles, coming together. Think of it like a magnet. I had always wondered how it would feel. So natural—easier than with two like powers—but a delicate balance. If I pull just a bit..."

Delilah leaned forward, the wonder on her face clouding.

"Interesting," Toa reflected. "Once linked, you can pull the focus of the magic. If you are not strong enough, or not knowledgeable enough, you will remain a pawn. I could use your magic, pulling through you. If I wasn't worried about your welfare, I could drain your energy easily. It is similar to a like-magic link, but with more trust. Less control. It is easier to maintain, but as such, easier to exploit."

Delilah leaned away, as if released, confusion and fear crossing her face.

Toa glanced at Sasha. "But your magic isn't exactly like theirs, Sasha. For you, a blood link is still better."

"Barking up the wrong tree, Toa. We've talked about that," Sasha said, face screwed up in concentration.

"Without a blood link, you can only rely on Stefan," Toa countered. "And let's not forget, links can be forced, blood or otherwise. You are exposed. All of you are exposed. We should pair everyone off, protect as much as we can here before we meet more of my kind. Not all are as gentle as this clan—they are not always as fair to humans."

Sasha snorted. "Goodie. And I do rely on Stefan. With my whole being. So stop asking."

"Who've I got?" Charles asked in wonder, wanting to reach forward and touch someone. He latched onto the link and pulled it toward him. Birdie leaned in, right before her face darkened and her eyebrows lowered. Before he knew what had happened, he was on his feet, the essence of flowers now a petal claw, grabbing his chest and yanking him. His energy sapped, his magic started to drain and close off.

Charles yanked back, magical tug-of-war, making Birdie grunt.

"She's an orange," Sasha said softly. "And bold. She's probably not afraid to club you, magically or otherwise."

Suddenly, the link was infused with a shot of magic. All four elements blasted into his body, slamming him back in his chair. His hands flew up, trying to shield him from something he couldn't see. Birdie gasped, her face alight with joy and terror.

As fast as it began, it stopped. Sasha slumped. "Same thing that happens with you, Toa," she said sadly. "My magic tries to fry everyone. Even my own kind."

Toa tapped his chin, his gaze losing focus. "You have all the elements, the polar opposite as me, but you are not controlling the flow. You fight the flow within you, not control it. You work with it in your own way, but you don't take ownership of it."

"Well, then, she needs a teacher, doesn't she?" Birdie stated. Her hands found her hips again, even though she was sitting. "If that's you, then you better figure it out. I've never seen such potential in my life."

"This is all really real?" one of the twins asked, staring at Jonas. "You feel like..."

"A crisp autumn day," the other twin helped, also looking at Jonas. "So beautiful and mild."

"You got the twins?" Charles whined. He always wanted to try twins. His kind didn't produce any that he knew of, and humans weren't much fun when they were all dopey-eyed.

"We need to learn to choose our linked partner, as well,"

Toa continued, still analyzing. "This is too loose. What we have done is without proper guidance."

"Nature doesn't conform to rules," Delilah noted. "And Jen's right—I can't believe this is happening! We'd always known we could call the corners—that they were real—but...this..."

"Yes, exciting," Toa waved her away. "I need to think about what I have learned here today. There are so many more issues than I originally thought. I do not want this exposure at the council."

His eyes glued to Sasha. "We haven't much time. Not at all. If only that mate of yours was in any way sane."

"You're one to talk," Sasha huffed.

"Yes, well." Toa stood, his glance at the ladies brief. "Thank you, everyone. This has been helpful. I will let Sasha fill you in on our kind. You have gifts, one and all. In fact, Sasha, define the magical levels for me, please. I find I cannot sense their power unless I merge with them."

She pointed at Birdie. "Orange. Raw power. But doesn't seem to have much finesse. Stefan wouldn't take her for the Watch. You know, if she could fight."

Delilah got a point. "Not much power, but really, really deft with it. She rode my coattails in the park and undid the last portion of that spell. So, that's handy. If you work out the linking thing, she'll be useful, I think."

Delilah preened. Charles wondered briefly if there was a wildcat under that mousy exterior.

"And the twins are topping at about red. But they work in tandem. They kind of always exist together. Somehow. Well, they all do. It's what I love. It's like holding hands."

Toa nodded, his suspicion confirmed probably. "Well, then. I'll leave you to your explanations. With such a large, dangling carrot, I cannot imagine they will turn down an opportunity to learn."

"A large, dangling carrot, Toa? Really?" Sasha commented dryly.

"Do I need to stay for the explanations?" Charles asked quickly.

"Yes. You're first watch." Jonas glanced at Sasha. "Call me if you run into problems, human."

Charles couldn't help the sigh. He crossed his arms over his chest and leaned further back in his chair. It would be a long afternoon.

"Jonas, be a lamb and grab my knitting, will you?" Charles said to the retreating figure, half mockingly.

"Stop being a bitch and get a man's hobby!" Jonas growled.

Yeah. That was about the response he expected.

CHAPTER FOURTEEN

"God, that Birdie can be demanding." I rubbed my eyes as I let myself into Stefan's and my living area. It had been a long, *long* day.

Birdie made me explain everything at least twice, in denial about all she was seeing. Even after I proved my magic again, and after Charles agreed with my explanations about his kind, she just had more questions. For a woman who thought computers were a passing fad, it made sense—change needed to be a gradual thing. But it was still more than a little frustrating.

"The other three were easy about it, for daft humans." Jonas loitered in the doorway, glancing around the empty area. "Where's the Boss?"

"You know, I can actually fend for myself once in a while. I don't always need a detail on me."

Jonas snorted, sauntering over to the couch and sitting down. Apparently that was him not believing me.

"What's the story with your mongrel friends?" Jonas threw a huge arm over the back of the couch as he got comfortable. "Haven't seen them around lately."

"You saw Ann yesterday."

"She doesn't count. What about that supposed head dick? What's he up to?"

Tim, he meant. God forbid he call Tim *alpha,* or even by his name—that would mean Tim had some clout.

I rolled my eyes and fell into the couch kitty-corner to Jonas. "He's had another shifter go missing. Ann said he was buckling down and checking the area. He doesn't want to involve me unless he has to."

"Doesn't want the Boss knowing about his movements, huh?"

"If he wanted to keep secrets from Stefan, he wouldn't tell me what was going on, genius. So no. But we all saw how you bunch of derelicts worked together—or *didn't* work together. Tim doesn't want to fight you if he wanders across a demon."

"You didn't see nothin'. Too busy making eyes at a demon."

"Ugh—your sense of humor is the pits. Ann filled me in."

Jonas scratched his nose and rested his hand on his bumpy stomach, more relaxed in this moment that I had seen him before. "I heard the demon situation yesterday went off easily. No mongrels present."

"Low-powered demon. When we need to use magic, we'll want the help of the shifters. Unless you idiots learn to trust them, and get out of the damn way, we'll always be crippled."

"That frosty-headed creep tell you about being able to talk to demons, yet?" Jonas asked, swinging his head my way conversationally.

It took a moment for those words to wind their way into my brain. It took another second to make sense of them. I went with the standard response in these situations. "Huh?"

"That's a no, then. Overheard them talking about it—him and the Regional. When someone calls a demon, apparently they have the language of the demon. They use that language, and their personal power, or some damn thing, to control it. If the demon's too strong, it can overtake the guy that summoned it. Kills him, usually. Probably why that cat ran the other day."

"As far as I know, and bear with me, because today was fairly hazy, but as far as I know, I haven't summoned a demon."

"No, but you can understand them. That means you got their language. *That* apparently means you can control them. Just have to assert your dominance."

"I see." I really didn't. "And I do this how?"

"Hell if I know. It all sounds absurd to me. Why would you want to mess around with them things? Kill it as fast as possible, that's my motto."

"Fascinating. Well thanks ever so much for bringing it up."

We passed a second in silence, a clock ticking somewhere in the distance, before he said, "Frosty is mystified by you, you know. You're throwing all sorts of weird shit at him and he can't come up with answers fast enough."

"Yeah. Weird shit seems to be my bag."

Jonas snorted. "Feeling sorry for yourself is just stupid. You landed the head honcho of this joint—something all the females have been after—got another head honcho as a new dad, got a real smart mage as your tutor, no matter how creepy... I'd say you got it made. Crying is just for sissies."

"So... don't look for pity handouts from you, then. Noted."

"All you gotta do is let your balls fly and lead this bitch. You got everything you need. Once you do that, everyone else will come around. Nothing to it."

I took out an imaginary pen and scribbled on the imaginary paper in my palm. "Let...my...balls...fly...and...lead...this...

bitch. Uh huh, got it. Sound advice, as always. Maybe a little too detailed, though."

Jonas snorted again and let his head fall back against the couch. "I'm not looking forward to that dang council meeting. It'll be nonstop fights. I hate when males try to throw their weight around."

"Not the females?"

He glanced at me sideways. "I like that, but in a different setting."

"Ah, right. So you're going, then?"

"Yeah. Gotta watch you. You'll get picked on, and Charles will definitely get picked on, young as he is, and I'll have to bust some heads."

"Sounds like your paradise."

He pointed his face toward the ceiling. "I will have to stop before I kill them."

"Ah. Yes, that sounds terrible." I couldn't stop from laughing. I liked this easy-does-it Jonas. His language skills were the pits, but he was actually kind of fun in a dry, everyone-is-an-idiot kind of way.

The door opened at the same time as my phone rang. I shot a smile toward Stefan and got a thick pulse of pleasure from the link—it was probably the same thing I was shooting at him. My eyes drifted toward the face of the phone where "Tim - alpha" was displayed in large white letters.

Wonderful timing, as ever.

"How'd it go with the witches?" Stefan asked as he slung a leather jacket across the nearest chair.

For a wonder, Jonas didn't bother getting up. It was testimony to how tired he was.

I gave Stefan a pointer finger to have him hold that thought as I answered the phone. "Hey, what's up?"

"Sasha? Tim. We got one."

A thrill went through my body. I sat up quickly, clutching the cold plastic to my ear. Stefan was beside me instantly.

"Got a demon? You've found another demon?" I clarified in anxious tones.

Jonas sat up next, a wave of violence washing over his body—you could tell by the quick flexing of his muscles.

"Yeah," came Tim's voice. "This one is a nasty one. We took out a different one yesterday—very low power. Sacrifice was a small animal and looked a day old. Didn't bother you with that one."

"Wait," I switched ears. "*You* took out a low-level demon yesterday? Because so did Stefan."

Tim snorted. "Figured he wouldn't call us."

Well, you didn't call him, either ...

I tapped my phone to speaker so everyone could hear. Stefan was already texting someone—probably Jameson.

"This clown is practicing," Tim said, "But he's here now. Can't see his face—he's hidden behind a blind, but he's here. He called up a nasty one, and he's getting ready to unleash it. It seems like he's waiting, though."

"Waiting for what?"

"Well..." the pause doused the room in silence for an anxious moment. "He called it on the same spot as Stefan's parents died."

So many emotions blasted through the link at once that I had to muffle it. Stefan stared at the phone, wide-eyed, fear warring the calm leader's mask he was trying for. Jonas stared at the ground, his arms falling into his lap limply.

"So he's waiting for Stefan, then," I clarified.

"Yup. Think so. And it's probably that guy Andris. We only got a glance at his body and the side of his head, but I could swear it was him."

"How many do we need?" I asked, as close to calm as I

could muster. With Stefan's swirling emotions and swinging mood, one of us had to stay level.

This would be interesting.

"One of my guys is calling this a class three. That is one bad mamma-jamma, Sasha. I got thirty people, all changed, surrounding it. We got might. We need magic."

I took a large breath. "We'll be there as soon as we can. Call if something changes."

"Yup." The screen went black as the other line disengaged.

My gaze rose slowly until I met those liquid black eyes filled with uncertainty. We were approaching the moment of truth, and Stefan barely held the reigns of control.

"Jonas," I said softly. "Go get Jameson. Start getting people ready. Stefan and I will be there in a minute."

Jonas jumped up. "You got it, mage."

Before he went through the door, I stopped him. "And Jonas?"

He turned and speared me with a haunted glance.

"Get the witches. We'll keep them way back, but we could use someone I can sorta link with."

Jonas nodded, shot a quick glance at Stefan, and then went through the door. Both men knew what I meant—someone I could link with in the event Stefan lost his nerve, shut down, and then unconsciously shut me out.

I faced the love of my life who was scared shitless for the third time ever. "I will be fine," I said.

His gaze locked on mine. He didn't acknowledge those words.

"Stefan, I will be fine. If we link, if you give me energy, I can knock that thing out. I know I can. I remember the strange spells from the warehouse, I know exactly how to cut out a *Dulcha,* I'm familiar with the intricacy of Andris' recent spells—all I need is a bunch of energy and some time. I can do this. I'll be safe."

Still his gaze held mine, his jaw clenched, his hands fisted. On the edge, battling his personal demons so hard he could barely focus on the real demon ready to be unleashed.

"What happened to your parents will not happen to me," I pushed softly. "This time, you will be there. You can help."

"I can't help if I'm taken from the fight, Sasha. We'll need Toa. There's still time to blood link with him. If we hurry, if we do it in the car, you can develop it. Or you can—"

I put a comforting hand on his bulging forearm. He clenched his jaw, fighting for control. Fighting the raging nightmare of his worst memory coming to life.

My heart went out to him, but I wouldn't let that thought filter into my gaze. He didn't need my compassion; he needed my strength.

"Okay. C'mon." I hauled him up, refusing to feel the butt tingle. Or the knee tingle. Or the goosebumps. Oh yeah, danger was waiting. I was walking, wide-eyed, into a situation that might kill me. And I couldn't even look terrified. Fan-freaking-tastic.

Outside the door we stalked, side-by-side, down the hall bustling with people. Stefan's face was a stern mask, nothing of his warring emotions bleeding through his hard expression. As far as everyone else could see, he was ready and deadly, in charge as usual.

We entered the weapon room where I snatched my protective leathers and my dagger. Jameson strolled in, leather duster billowing out behind him. He had the same stern mask Stefan did, but his wasn't as watertight. Cracks of fear and uncertainly flashed across his expression. "Boss, mage."

I spared him a glance as I snatched my lucky whistle off its hook. "We're going to make it through this just fine."

He started, doing a double take, and honed in on me. It was hard to mistake the pleading in his hazel eyes. And then, slightly embarrassed, he nodded hastily and turned back to Stefan.

"Boss, I've got twenty strong here. I've got ten more I'm pulling in from the field. Then I've got a group of five magic users, all the best. I've also got some humans Jonas is claiming Sasha asked for on the way. I've notified the Regional. He is letting you and Sasha take lead."

Stefan attached his dagger to his side. "Sasha and Toa will make up the chief source of magic to take the demon out. I will balance them, along with the witches. The magic users you collected will be a wall between the demon and them. The warriors will be the front line. We protect the magic users. If those animals turn tail and run, we protect our own."

Jameson's eyes hardened. "Who else do you want to link with, Sasha and Toa?"

Stefan slid into his vest, leather hugging his large upper body tightly. He shrugged into his leather duster. "They won't need anyone else besides the witches. Probably couldn't accept anyone else. Between the two of them ... and myself, we'll have a stack of magic and energy both. It should be enough. But..." I got a glance. "The mage has the final say on that."

"You're going to hang back with them?" Jameson asked in an almost-level tone.

A muscle in Stefan's jaw throbbed as it clenched and unclenched. "I am the only one that can balance Sasha's power. Without me, she cannot link with anyone."

I tried not to notice the accusatory glance Jameson shot me. My heart sank. I was taking Stefan away from the fight, from his vengeance. From him making his past right.

I took another deep breath. This was no time for second-guessing. His presence would be more valuable on my end.

"Those merges are set. Ready?" I pushed.

We made our way through the house and out the front door to a waiting team of idling cars. Jonas and Charles joined me immediately, fierce-eyed and grim-faced. Toa drifted up out of nowhere, Dominicous right behind.

"Sasha, this is a powerful demon. The one who summoned it—"

"Let's do this in the car," I cut Toa off. "We need to get there."

Jonas crawled into the driver's seat of his Hummer, and Stefan followed into the front passenger seat, simmering. He was keeping it together, but emotion ripping at him. Pushing, pulling. Half of him felt like a little kid, scared and uncertain. The other a warring man, ready to tear into this thing that threatened his way of life. The link put it all out there, showing me his every emotion. His face showed none of it.

I swallowed past the lump in my throat. This was real. Really, really real.

"Okay, Toa, what were you saying?" I asked as Charles whisked Dominicous into another ride.

"The one who summoned the demon is on site, and he will be giving commands. The demon will be trying to break free, however. Always trying to break free. It will speak to you. I haven't told you this—"

"I can speak to them, yes, I know," I cut Toa off again. "Jonas told me."

Toa's lips made a thin line across his face. "Jonas the expert, yes. And did he, perhaps, tell you *how* you can assume control?"

"No, and I doubt I'll be able to learn now, while also trying to link, while also trying to cut it out of this world."

"Don't try to assume control, no. That is a lesson for another day—one I am still reading up on. But you need to try and discourage it from connecting with you. You don't want it to get in your head. They have been known to steal the power of their supposed masters. As one that can speak to it, you will be a potential master in its eyes."

"It won't be any different than normal, though, right?" I qualified, my butt tingle getting decidedly more pronounced the closer we got to the site.

I wanted to roll down the window and jump out of the moving vehicle. Then, after I rolled to a bloody stop, I wanted to hobble away as fast as possible. My inner sense said heading into this danger was the worst possible decision I could possibly make. It made concentration difficult.

"This one has more power," Toa answered, cool as a spring day. "Its words will be harder to tune out."

"Great. Should be a hoot."

We rolled to a stop amid a sea of vehicles. Charles and Dominicous were getting out beside us, both ignoring the gaggle of witches filing out of the car as well. The people in my car didn't move.

I watched the witches through the window crowd around Charles, demanding answers.

"We're here," I said into the quiet car.

"Yes," Toa responded.

"Cover the link, Sasha," Stefan said in a low tone.

"But Stefan—"

"Cover the link." He looked back, power and command shocking into me.

I took another big breath as fear and uncertainty muffled, and then disappeared from my body. Well, Stefan's fear anyway—I still had plenty of my own.

I searched down deep for the other link, the faint one left over from when I was a child in shock. When I found it, I nearly gasped. Impatience, anxiety, and yes, fear warring through his center, spiking and rolling.

Amazed, I jerked my vision toward him, on the other side

of Charles' car. There Dominicous stood, face firm and resolute, his strength and power expressing his utter confidence.

It was good to know my fear wasn't abnormal—I was just worse at hiding it. Or ignoring it.

"Ready, Sasha?" Stefan asked in bold tones. He was getting ready to lead.

"She nodded," Toa helped, climbing gracefully from the car.

I clambered out as well, feeling the adrenaline start to pique through my limbs. I opened up and let the elements flow, washing over me. Immediately the *wrongness* of the magic in the area accosted me, magical sludge covering me in filth.

"This place doesn't feel right," Delilah said softly as she stepped closer. The others came over as well. "Something not good awaits us."

Large warriors stepped around us, making their way to the battle zone. All the guys with us except Jonas and Charles did the same, getting in position, coming up with a plan.

"Call the corners right now," I addressed the group of women. "Stay connected."

I turned to stare directly at Birdie. "If the demon breaks through, you need to run. Get out of here, okay? Take the girls with you."

Her chin rose a fraction. "Absolutely not. You've been at this for a few months. I've been at this for a few decades. I will not turn tail if you need me."

The others nodded, less certain, but not cowards. And that was the thing with women. We could show our fear, and admit to being terrified, but when someone was in need, we pushed that aside and showed up to the party.

I exhaled a breath I didn't know I was holding. "Stupid move, but okay."

"Mage." A steadfast man, short for his race at only six-foot-one or so, stared down at me with a severe face. He looked vaguely familiar, but so did everyone. I was having a hard time remembering what duty everyone had.

"Yes?"

"I'm Zeke. Chief magical user, specializing in linking. I'll be leading the magical unit to protect you."

"Oh. Thanks." What else was I supposed to say? *Yes, I should've remembered you of all people. Sorry about that. Also, thanks for putting your life on the line for someone that completely forgot your duty.*

I really needed to start doing flashcards with faces and names!

As if on cue, a cluster of men and women pushed in behind him, ready to follow me to the front line and battle with magic. And somehow, it felt way different than battling the Eastern Territory. For one, we weren't squaring off against people with the same caliber of fighting—we were squaring off against an otherworldly creature. Second, everyone was scared shitless. I could see it in the tiny movements and the shifty eyes.

For them to be afraid—a warrior race who thrived on battles—meant this was a very bad situation.

"Suck it up, child. There is a job to be done." Birdie patted me on the back, the last touch being a small shove.

Summoning my courage, I marched out beyond the cars, magical people at my back. Jonas and Charles waited for me, falling in beside me as I passed.

"Ready for this, Sasha?" Charles asked quietly.

I nodded. I didn't trust my voice.

A line of huge warriors spread out before me, standing firm on scarred and burnt grasses. Swords glowed at sides and tattoos peeked out of battered and stressed leather. Off to the left was a group of trees holding some sort of cloth hanging within its branches. The wind, slight but present, billowed the material, catching on leaves. A flickering glow from within half silhouetted a large figure, still for the moment.

That had to be the guy who summoned the demon.

"Why don't we go and rip that loser out of the trees?" I asked the cluster around me.

"He is within the confines of his spell. If we cross his barrier, it will release the demon." Toa drifted up, sparing only a quick glance for the magic people behind me. "We have two objectives here tonight. One, take down the demon. Obviously, this is first. Two, capture whoever is calling them. He will be tied here while the demon is in existence—a stronger demon has a stronger hold on the caster. One of this magnitude will bind him, I am sure. If he loses hold for even one moment, he will be in a fight for his life, just as we are. When we banish the creation, we will hope to have enough manpower alive to go after the creator."

"Always with the sugar-and-flower delivery, Toa," I commented, my arms shaking so bad I had to clasp my hands together. "A real encourager, you are."

"You sound like Yoda. Come on." Charles put his hand on my back to steer me, something he did when he knew my courage was dicey. The warmth of his hand seeped into my skin, comforting me a little. Worst came to worst, he wouldn't leave me.

As I neared the cluster of warriors, a hole formed in their wall of muscle. For the first time, I could see across the field. The rays of the nearly full moon fell across a huge, winged creation, looking surprisingly like...

"Is that an angel?" I asked in a wispy voice.

"A weeping angel," Stefan answered in a growl. "It's merely the form it took."

"But...it looks sweet and innocent."

Standing within the confines of a large circle drawn in the ground by what looked like oil, but was most assuredly blood, stood a slender woman-figure in billowing robes. A band or wreath of some kind circled her head, trapping short blondish curls to her scalp. A serene expression stared out of a porcelain face. Large, feathery black wings curled up behind it.

"That's just not right," I reflected.

Beyond the circle, standing twenty yards away on what must be their territory, was a half-circle of fur. Animals of all varieties had lined up and spread out with a huge bear in the middle, staring across at us. Tim and his crew were ready to fight, waiting on my signal.

"Okay, let's get this party underway." Stefan glanced to his right and left, his warriors taking his signal and immediately falling into formation. A line stretched out along the circle on our half of the territory line, swords hanging low and ready, the colors of red through burnished gold.

"But if we just cover one side, and the Shifters run," I commented softly, "which they won't, but if they did, the demon would just run that way and escape. I thought you would try to double-cover..."

"Andris is controlling this demon," Stefan informed me in a tight voice. "It will come for me. After it kills me, it will try to take you, most likely. Trek didn't know much, but he was under the impression Andris could bend you to his will if I were out of the picture."

"Well, Trek has always been a little delusional. The cape should've told you that."

"And we don't have enough people to double-cover," Stefan went on. "We have to focus on what's important. You."

The fabric within the tree saw movement and pushed to the side. The angel in the center of the circle looked slowly to her right. And out walked Andris, cool and calm, sporting a small smile on his relaxed face.

His eyes found, and then stuck to, Stefan. His smile grew. "We meet again."

"Which was your intention," Stefan returned. "You've been practicing."

"Of course. You know me; I like to get it right before I use my knowledge to its full potential."

"But you didn't get it right with Trek."

Soft laughter echoed across the clearing. "Not yet. He's a fool, but a useful one. And you've kept him safe and sound for me, thank you for that. I will pick up that project after this. With all your magic workers here, who is left to protect your homestead?"

"We've always had more talent than you, Andris. We have plenty more magic workers at the mansion, and more still in other outcroppings."

"Yes, but not the best. Speaking of—" His honey-spun eyes flashed to me. "Sasha, so good of you to come. Do you think you're ready for this?"

"I have a white mage, too." I jerked a thumb at Toa. "And your practicing has really helped my understanding of how these little suckers exist. I can blink this thing out lickity-split."

"Are you so sure?" Andris asked in a silky voice.

Nope. I absolutely wasn't. Especially in the face of all that confidence. But he didn't have to know that.

"Let's get the show on the road," I drawled. "I'm not in the mood for drawing things out."

"Of course."

A flare of brilliant orange lit up the clearing, a translucent circle shimmering around the demon. Its face turned straight again, its eyes glancing from one face to the next. When it got to mine, it stopped. A tiny smile quirked plump lips.

"A power play among masters. But you are so young. Such a young, pretty thing." The words tickled my ears and seduced my senses. They sparkled and shimmered, wrapping me up and sucking all of my focus toward it. I didn't want to look away. I didn't want to breathe. I only wanted to listen. "I will enjoy feasting on your young flesh."

"What, no riches and wealth of power?" I asked sardonically, barely hearing my own voice, my magic pushing into that circle and feeling around the spells contained there.

"I have no need of riches. I have my own wealth of power. But, oooh, your magic feels nice. Clean. Uncorrupted. Yes, a good feast it will be."

"Sasha..."

The name flapped around my head, trying to work into my consciousness. My name. Someone was calling me.

"Sasha."

I could barely turn my head with the draw of the being in the center of the circle. My gaze, hating to be away from that soft, glowing face, focused on a pair of onyx eyes, squinted with worry.

Stefan.

My heart leaped, trying to connect with that other half. My other half. Trying to find solace within him.

My mind bowed, ripped away toward a new focus. The mists cleared from my thoughts. I stared at that impossibly handsome face.

"Stick with me, baby," Stefan said earnestly. "Stick with me."

In a flare of light that had all the warriors flinching, the circle fluxed ... and winked out. Everyone braced.

Mayhem.

Huge black wings spread out behind the demon, oil slicked and holey. A loud screech, like a bird of prey, erupted from its throat. Fangs grew from its mouth as claws elongated from its fingers.

"Kill him!" Andris pointed directly at Stefan.

The shifters lurched forward, growls and snarls drowning out the seething beast within that circle. Stefan's warriors pushed forward, swords held high. Stefan stepped with them, shoving me behind him.

The line of magic workers filed in front of me the next instant, blocking me off. Dividing me from Stefan. Flashes of pale gold light zinged toward the demon, shimmering before molting into black and singeing away.

Another screech.

The demon's claws ripped out and sliced, tearing a throat from a badger. The wings, fluttering now, slashed and maimed anything it touched, as if the ends were made of razor blades. Animals and men both fell to the sides, blood splashing the air-riding clumps of flesh and fur, as the demon shredded through the crowd.

Stefan rushed forward, his sword out, no longer directing people, focused solely on his enemy. He knew it challenged him, and he rose to meet that challenge head-on.

"We must blood link!" Toa shouted above the din. He grabbed my arm and hauled me backward. "We must link! Stefan is lost. He is manic—*look* at him!"

The angel turned, her decrepit wings spreading out behind her, one tearing through Stefan's duster, slicing a line of red into his back. He ripped off the leather, huge muscled arms swirling with white-crusted gold. Movements silky and graceful despite the awe-inspiring power and strength, he charged through the fight, violence and destruction, leading by example.

But Toa was right—his face, like that of Jonas and Jameson, was single-minded focus infused with pain. His head—all their heads—probably flashed with memories. With nightmares. The things that woke him up screaming were the things he was battling now. In the flesh. Without me.

I glared at Toa, wild-eyed. "We don't have time for a blood link. What about Dominicous? Can I focus on that?"

"We could never pull him out in time!" Toa pointed to my new father, deep in the fray, fighting right alongside Stefan. Battle rage had taken over the lot of them. This was how they dealt with attacks, leaving the magic workers to sort out the rest.

But the magic workers weren't enough. Without me able to link, we'd have to rely on the other circle—except, they fought their huge flux of magic between them, their fear making the link unstable. Their magic worked too slowly—by the time they cut out the demon, most of Stefan and Tim's men would be dead, including my future mate, my new father, and all my new friends.

"Shit!" I yelled, frustrated and terrified.

"I am coming for you, young one," I heard above the screams and shrieks. My heart beat unnecessarily fast. My attention wandered. "I will have you. *Join me*."

CHAPTER FIFTEEN

Like an intense orgasm, a jolt of pure pleasure rocked my body. I sucked in a shocked breath.

"Join me!"

All my fear melted away. A soothing sort of tranquility blanketed me, singing softly, laughing in a perfect pitch. A voice tickled my ears, "I will have you. Wait there for me. I am coming."

"Yes." My smile must've taken up my whole face. I wanted this—to connect myself with that presence. It made me feel so *alive*. So...beautiful.

"Come to me, young one," the voice called to me.

"Yes!" I said again, dreamily. Sparks of joy lit up my body, erased all my worries, all my fears. All that awaited was pleasure. Pleasure, and power.

So much power. I could almost feel it, sucking me forward. Trying to merge with me and share this wonderful magic that filled up my body.

Why had everyone warned me away from this? This was *heaven!* Absolute bliss!

"Come to me."

Of course I will, I thought to myself. I have to. No...I *need* to.

I laughed, so hard. I couldn't help it. I felt so good. So light. Like that first plunge of delicious, sinful sex. The hot and cold of desire. The slow burn of intercourse.

"Open the link!"

I blinked at the words yelled into my face. They sounded so coarse. So disgusting. So filthy and human.

"Open the link!"

I pushed at the face—a striking face. Attached to a large body, brimming with power. More power. I could take from him so easily—he'd link with me. He'd trust me.

I turned to Charles, a sweet smile on my face, a hot fire in my loin. I grabbed his neck and pulled him down to my lips, my magic assaulting his, trying to enact the link while my hands explored his body. He held me close as he yelled, *"Damn it, Sasha. No! Open the link!"*

Without thinking, certainly not meaning to, that muffle pulled off of the link, revealing another power source. I felt the demon laugh, a pleasing lick up my bones—so much power. I had so much of my own, and access to so much more.

"Well done, young one."

My gaze rose to the battlefield, taking in my instructions. Watching in awe as the angel spun and twisted, so full of deadly grace. So beautiful.

As I was about to pull away, to drain this man I was held firmly against, a head stuck in my way. Onyx eyes shocked into me, searing my bliss. Something rose through my core, ripping at that consuming pleasure. Trying to sever the link with the angel.

"No!" I screamed, trying to clutch on.

That blissful longing was wrestled by something else.

Something fierce and possessive. Something to match the angel's power.

"Take his power!" the angel commanded.

Panting, snarling, I wrestled with that force inside of me. I tried to hold onto the high of orgasm; the sinful pleasure curling around my body. But something else had welled up. With damning force, something else was ripping me toward it. And then a dull throb took over, rocking me for a second time, but then cradling me as well.

Love.

Stefan.

Like bubbles popping, the haze started to dissolve. The sinful effulgence of a moment before rotted. The night descended once again, slashing out the dream of paradise only gotten through death.

I sucked in what felt like the first big breath of my life. I maintained contact with those liquid black eyes as he took a step; a painful, agonizing step, away from his battle. Away from his vengeance. Toward me.

"Kill him!" the creature screeched.

Stefan's lips moved, no sound reaching me, but what he said was easy to recognize. "You're mine."

Another blast of intense love pumped through the blood link. Powerful strides now, away from the creature that had shaped his past. To me, the person that would help shape his future. "Stay with me, baby," he said.

A tear rolled down my cheek as I fell into his commanding stare. Sank into his presence through the blood link. Gave myself over to him completely.

"Shake it off, baby," he stated from directly in front of me now. He grabbed my face as he trapped my gaze. "*You're mine!* Shake it off, and send it away!"

I fell into that command. I focused on those eyes. I felt

that pulsing deep in my body, responding to him. Needing him.

At one with him.

I took a shuddering breath.

A disgusting screech of frustration shook the battlefield.

"There is no time! We must link!" Toa yelled. "I don't have the power to do it without her!"

Stefan threaded his fingers through mine. "This is your show, love. Take it home."

The demon's call was still there, beckoning me, trying to bring my focus toward it. But now Stefan shielded me, blanketing me in his protection, holding my focus to him with steadfast strength. I took comfort in his power and energy as it bled through the link, and then felt the sisterhood behind me, begging me to join. And Toa, to my right, waiting impatiently for me to be ready. I closed my eyes as the girls whisked me up into their fold, unity and strength. Togetherness. I was not alone.

Toa said to Stefan, indecision fighting necessity, "Link with me. Then let her bring you in."

Suddenly our link pulsed, a lot of power on my doorstep, but that was nothing new. The difference was the amount of energy. I felt massive, colossal, more powerful than I could even imagine, able to work an exponential amount of power.

I sucked in the elements. Not opened up to them like usual, *sucked* at them. Within seconds my body was full to bursting. Hot spikes of pain spread across my limbs.

"Okay, Stefan ..."

His special gift worked through me, balancing, moving magic around, leveling everything out.

"Amazing," Toa breathed to the side.

"Whoa," one of the twins said.

"Now, go get 'im!" Birdie pushed.

I shoved my magic toward the circle the creature stepped

out of, feeling the magic there, born from blood. Lots of blood, too, woven tightly with intricate detail. I focused, feeling the structure of the spells within the lacy framework until I felt down to the root; that little cord I'd found with that first demon, connecting it from its home to this world. I had no idea how it worked, but I knew that if I segregated the spell connected to that spot, light's out for Mr. Demon.

"Here we go," I murmured, focusing.

I picked at it as fast as I could, peeling back one spell and moving aside another, trying to get at that root. Sweat dripped down my face as my body burned through energy.

Stefan worked right along with me, feeding me energy as he tried to not only balance the Merge he was heading, which included Toa, Charles and the witches, but keep my endless stream of power from blasting through the link to him. He managed it, though, as only he could, keeping me balanced, feeding me energy, and keeping my magic from overriding him.

One in a million, as Toa often said.

I felt the whispered sigh as another spell dissolved into elements, returning to nature. The demon's power dropped a notch. I struggled with the next one, weaves so detailed it could've been art, until it, too, bled into the night.

"Almost," I whispered. "One left."

As if it heard me, the demon's head snapped up, noticing its loss of power. It screeched, a disconnected limb waggling in its hand. Blood dripped down its face and body as it honed in on me.

"Hurry," Toa cried, sinking to his knees with the strain. I wasn't far behind him.

"Delilah, help," I murmured, trying to figure out how the spell was put together. Like trying to find the end of clear tape, I couldn't get a grip. I couldn't figure out where to pull to unravel it.

Deft magical hands moved over mine. Only a little power, but not needing it, Delilah felt along the spell. Traced it. Learned it.

"Intricate," she breathed. "Like the one at the park, but more advanced."

"If you can't unravel it, you must sever it," Toa said.

"That will kill those around it," Stefan argued. "Work at it, Sasha. You can do it."

I held the power, bleeding it into Delilah slowly as she worked, managing it for her. Power wasn't the problem, though. It was the energy. The massive amounts of energy it took to unravel this spell. To banish this thing.

"Why is it sucking so much energy?" I pleaded. "We aren't casting."

"You are casting," Toa panting. "You are reversing the spell without the use of sacrifice. Without the power of a life-force."

"You are the power of the life-force," Stefan clarified.

Delilah found a small rough patch that let her get in and start to disentangle. "I got it," she grunted, working at it, leading me, and then helping me; teamwork.

We started to unravel, our magic working around each other, bumping off of each other, but not forcing a link. Unity in like-power.

"I...don't..." Toa's head bowed. Stefan bent over at the waist, barely holding me up. Birdie hit the ground, followed by the twins. Charles went to one knee.

"Almost," I said, feeling the last of it. A couple more fibers, so lacy. So hard to identify.

A bloody glob flew over us, followed by a limp body.

It was one of the magic workers.

My gaze snapped into focus.

Face screwed up in a terrifying mask of rage, the demon ran at us, bodies strewn in its wake.

"Kill them!" Andris shouted somewhere off to the side, as if it needed to be said.

"Oh god!" I breathed, my body shaking.

My magic touch shook as hard as my body. The elements raged at me. Stefan struggled to contain it all.

"Easy does it, love. Easy does it. Focus," he said in a strained voice.

The wings on the demon snapped out behind it, holey black things with razor sharp edges. Its claws gleamed, dripping with blood. It ran, thirty feet away and running fast.

Panic flooded me.

I started to pant. Four more strings. I'd never make it in time!

"Run, you guys!" I urged. "Run away!"

"Cut it off!" Toa yelled.

Jonas hastened in around it, limping, blood running in deep rivulets down his chest. Jameson joined him a moment later, yanking at the wings to pull it back; to slow it down. They tried to tackle it, razor sharp wings and all.

"Hurry, love!" Stefan said, trying to stand in front of me, his voice rising.

The demon wiped its hand through the air, catching Jameson and flinging his body ten feet. Jonas slashed with his sword, catching the thick hide of the chest but not causing much damage.

I toiled as fast as I could, working at it, feeling my energy suck out of my body, knowing it was down to the last.

Three more strings. I had to disentangle three more.

Jonas screamed. His body crumpled at the demon's feet.

"Oh no!" I cried, working faster. Almost done. Two more strings.

A bear bellowed, two huge arms spreading out behind the demon and then clamping down, hugging it brutally, trapping the wings to its body. A mountain lion limped around to the front of it—Ann! Her back leg was tucked protectively into her body, the bone sticking out at the knee.

Sweat dripped into my eye. My breath roared in my ears. My limbs felt like useless weights. So tired. I was so tired.

Stefan hit a knee, pulling me closer. "Almost there, baby. Hang on."

Spikes of pain were flaring now, all of us holding too much magic without the energy reserves to support it.

"One more," I said, my voice nothing more than a hoarse release of breath.

The demon twisted around and stuck its claws in Tim's furry stomach. It ripped upward. Tim bellowed, trying to hold on as the claws went in a second time.

"No, Tim!" I cried, struggling to keep going. His large furry body collapsed to the ground.

Choking through tears, I kept working—the spell was laid now, the finish line in view.

The demon faltered. Its life line was weakening, but it was so powerful. So, *so* much power.

The cry of a mountain lion cut through the night, Ann now the only thing in the way.

"Run, Ann!" I yelled. It came out as a hoarse whisper.

My vision blurred and clouded as I pinched apart the last thread. Energy rushed out to disintegrate the last of the spell. Ann sailed through the air.

We didn't have enough energy to banish that final spell. It wouldn't be enough.

Ann was braced, teeth ready, ready to give her life.

"No, please," I begged. Stefan fell to two knees, not able to keep standing.

We didn't have enough.

Panicked, gasping, I snatched at that weak blood link. Focused on it. And then tugged with everything I had, trying to make the bridge between us bigger through sheer will alone. Begging for more. Begging not for my life, but Stefan's, and Toa's, and Ann's—begging for just a bit more energy so I could wipe out this demon once and for all.

Faint and hurting, I felt him, struggling to get up. He didn't have much left, but he recognized who I was and what I was asking.

Sweet, pure energy bled through our link. Dominicous, my dad, had come to my aid.

Hot tears stung my face as the energy was sapped back out again, fulfilling the spell's requirements. Unraveling what Andris had constructed.

I looked up just as Ann's body leapt for the demon.

"No, Ann!" I screamed. "I've done it. No!"

Ann's body fell onto the demon, her teeth sinking into its neck. It screeched, reaching up with bloody claws, jabbing into her jugular.

"No!" I yelled again.

Andris screamed, a blood-curdling wail of pain, cut short. Wings flapped like holey ship sales in front of us, until finally, *finally* the terrible creature imploded. It winked out, a wash of sludge and slime coating Ann as she fell to her side.

"We did it," Toa panted. "We did it."

CHAPTER SIXTEEN

I woke up to filtered light through the window, the sun just sinking below the horizon. My alarm clock shrilled a second later. I gave it a good slap and sat up. Then groaned.

"Still sore?" Stefan asked, turning on his side to regard me.

I traced his big shoulder muscle and smiled. "A bit. Literally all I did was stand around and work some magic, but it feels like I ran to the moon and back. It's been a week—I feel like I should be healed by now."

I slunk out of bed and ambled toward the big bay window at the side of the room. I pushed aside the heavy curtain, enjoying the beautiful oranges and pinks that lit up the sky. "I've always loved sunsets."

"Hmm." Stefan climbed out of bed and closed the distance between us, snaking his arms around my middle. He kissed my cheek and stared out with me, savoring the moment.

"What's on the agenda today?" I asked softly, sinking into his brawny embrace.

"Check in with the wounded, mourn the loss of those that didn't make it, and dinner. With me."

I turned my head so I could rest my face against his. "I need to check in with the *Mata,* too."

Stefan remained silent. It had been only one week since that demon tore through our world, but it was long enough for Stefan to start to come to grips with his past. The biggest problem had been reassessing the shifters.

Not one of the *Mata* had fled. Not a single one. They fought bravely right alongside our clan. Because of that, Stefan no longer grumbled when I went to visit, or snarled when they came here, but old haunts took a while to dissipate. The best he could do right now was keep his silence. And he did. Baby steps.

His lips trailed up my neck until he captured my lips. He deepened the kiss, spicy and wild. When he backed off I was breathless.

"Did I mention dinner would be served in a hot tub? And we'd be naked?" he asked in his deep rumble.

"Or...eat, and *then* have sex in the tub."

He chuckled and released me. "Fair enough."

After a hot shower and some clothes, we emerged from our room. Charles sat on the couch, his haphazard and misshapen quilt stretched out on his lap. He glanced up as we walked in. "Ready?"

"Yeah." I looked at Stefan. "You coming with me, or are you doing your own thing?"

"My own thing? You mean, leading this clan with a steel fist?"

"Yes, honey, leading this clan with a steel fist." I patted his elbow.

"And a huge set of brass balls!" Charles joined in.

"Oh god, don't get the adolescent started. He'll never stop." I made my way to the door, the boys right behind me.

Stefan held the door for me. "I'll be with you today. I think we should do these duties together."

We'd lost a quarter of our troop, one of those being Claudia. Adnan took that one pretty hard, even though he hadn't known her well. The *Mata* had lost about the same amount, including Jack, the Tiger who had saved my life in the past. Of the survivors, most were wounded in some way. That demon, what they classed as a two after it was all said and done, tore through people, virtually indestructible. It had nearly overcome Andris even as it was trying to assume control of me. Without us to stop it, it would've gone on, killing and destroying. We were lucky not many had the power, know-how, and magic to call one that powerful. We were also lucky that Dominicous was able to grab Andris before he crawled away.

Literally.

Speaking of Dominicous. I felt his unmistakable serenity as he came around the corner in front of us, Toa by his side. The man was a cool breeze, until he was a hot furnace. He seemed to switch on and off like a light.

While his link to me wasn't nearly as strong as mine and Stefan's, or his and Toa's, it was enough to get the general point across. Being that I could mask it at any time, Stefan was mostly okay with the connection, especially since the paperwork had been filled out. In this culture, he was legitimately my father.

And that connection came with Toa. It could be worse.

"Sasha. Stefan. Hello." Toa bowed his blond head with a serious scowl in place he didn't bother hiding. He was less refined around Stefan and me since I became Dominicous' rightful heir. I had no idea why, but it was actually a nice change. Expressions were good, even though the lectures were still boring as hell—when I listened, obviously.

Dominicous grinned and nodded his hello as they passed

—he'd taken a hard knock to the throat with a pair of claws. He still had the nasty gouge marks. While that was healing, he didn't say much. Unfortunately, that meant Toa had the run of the mill with the lectures.

Somehow, it could be worse.

"What's up Toa's butt this time?" I asked as they wandered away slowly.

"Same old debate, I think—Toa is still pushing to blood link with you. Where, before, Dominicous was on board, now with his link to you, he doesn't feel it's needed. I agree, obviously. Toa's not pleased we are all ganging up on him."

"He knows I wouldn't agree, anyway. Why is he still pushing?"

"If he can get Dominicous and I to agree, he thinks we can talk you into it."

I laughed as we made our way down the stairs. "All this so he doesn't have to link through you, is that it?"

"Exactly. He still doesn't trust me."

"I don't think he trusts anybody," Charles offered. "That guy needs to go find a book to stick his nose in. He frets too much. Tries to hide it, but hang around him awhile, and you'll see it."

We entered the rooms dedicated to the wounded—those that needed care more often. These were the men and women hurt the worst, and without the ability to take care of themselves quite yet. All were on the mend, though. All would make it.

I knew exactly which bed I was visiting first.

"I don't need you visiting every day, human," Jonas growled, staring at the ceiling. "And when can I get out of this damn place? I'm sick of being here."

Charles leaned toward the bed over me. "The day you can wipe your own ass, bro, is the day I give a shit."

I gave Charles an elbow to shut him up. "How are you feeling?"

"Like shit. How do you think?" Jonas responded.

"How you look, then. You feel exactly how you look."

I elbowed Charles again as Jonas' gaze swung over, promising retribution.

"Just sayin', bro." Chuckling, Charles wandered away to visit someone else.

"You did good, though," I said to Jonas seriously. "You fought a good battle."

Jonas returned his gaze to the ceiling.

"I'm glad that attempt to kill me that one time failed ..."

It was a joke. Judging by the stare, he didn't care.

"So...do you need anything?"

"You to fuck off," Jonas growled.

"Well that's not very nice."

"You know I hate when people see me...in this place. You just come by to rub it in."

I thought about it for a second. "Yeah, that's true. Oh hey, and also, there's a new bumper sticker on your car. You'll see it when you feel better. I think it really fits."

A glare followed me as I walked away. There wasn't a new bumper sticker, but he didn't know that. Payback's a bitch for all those times he was way too cranky.

After we said a few words to the sick people, and called in on the more mobile people that got to go back to their rooms, we headed toward the car. Stefan would be visiting the *Mata* with me, because he owed them that much.

As we walked down the hall, people around us cleared, as usual. Stefan got his usual nods of deference, with the occasional, "Boss," thrown in. Not as usual, I had started getting noticed, too. Not by everyone, but at least half of those we saw connected eyes with me. They lowered their heads, and often said, "Mage."

"Word is getting around. You played your part. You led the link and succeeded where a magical unit of five couldn't," Stefan said in a low voice, for my ears alone. "They've accepted you in this position, but now they are accepting you as one of their guardians."

I couldn't help the delighted smile.

"Next step, one of them. A human. What has the world come to?" Charles chuckled behind us.

"That was a private conversation," Stefan growled back him.

"Sorry, Boss. My bad."

We made our way to the *Mata* community, a sprawling set of houses tucked away on a lot of acreage. This wasn't the place I had stayed to learn, it was normal houses removed from the city somewhat. We parked and made our way to the main house.

With my heart in my chest, I nodded to Ralph, the guy watching the door, and turned down a small hallway. At the end, the door was open. Barely breathing, I peeked my head inside.

Tim lay on the bed, pale and drawn, lacerations grooved down his chest. But his chest was still rising and falling. Shallow, but working.

"Hey," Ann said as she hobbled over on crutches. Shifters healed extremely quickly, but some of these people sustained serious injuries. Just like with the clan members, it would take a while.

"How is he?" I asked softly.

Stefan shifted in the doorway.

Ann shrugged. "He's okay. They say he's out of harm's way. He'll make it."

A huge breath rushed out of me. I sagged against Stefan. "Thank god. And how are you?"

She grimaced. "My. Leg. *Itches!* This cast is terrible!"

I laughed as she slowly led us outside. She'd felt the pricks of the demon's claws, but because big cats had such thick fur around their necks, and because I'd cut out the spell when I did, she only sustained four deep grooves in her neck. They'd scar, but she was alive.

She led us outside and to the right, sitting down on a stone bench and closing her eyes. "Goddamned Andris. What the hell was he thinking summoning something like that?"

"He has always been ambitious," Stefan offered noncommittally.

Ann rolled her eyes and leaned back. "Well, anyway, how are your troops? How's Jonas? Still grumpy?"

I shrugged. "Yep, surly as ever. Still in bed."

A haunted look passed over her face, but was gone in a flash. She wasn't one to dwell—generally being a pretty happy person. The memories with the demon would take effort, but she was working on it. "And the witches?"

Stefan snorted and walked away some, taking himself for a walk. Charles, who was waiting by the car, walked over to join him. As he passed us, he pinned Ann with a stare. "Hi. I'm fine, too, by the way. In case you wanted to know."

"I didn't," she shot back, watching him. Her mouth twisted up in a smile as she refocused on me.

"They're demanding to be taught. Which they will be, of course. Birdie is an orange, which is huge for a human. Delilah can get better, too, if she learns. And one of the twins has a kid, so everyone loves when they visit," I answered.

"So they're going to start learning?"

I nodded, feeling the chill in the air as winter drifted closer. "I'm crossing my fingers that they'll get really good. So I can have a bigger foothold."

Ann laughed and sat up. "Just keep working at it. You're not one to give up."

"Hey, Ann?"

She glanced over.

"Thanks," I gushed softly. "For trying to protect me. Again. Probably should've said it before now, but...I'm an ass, what can I say."

She grinned and shrugged at the same time. "You were trying to save all our butts. Least I could do."

Stefan and I did have our dinner that night. We ate at the table, like normal people, before we stripped naked and jumped into the hot waters. I felt complete in a way I never had before. Grounded and loved. I had lost myself to that demon, but he did as he said, and shielded me. Protected me, and then brought me back to reality. I didn't really care what happened with this job, or the house, or anything, as long as it was him and me. Us together, my new friends, and my father to back us up, meant I had somewhere solid to call home for the first time since I lost my parents. I had a family.

_*_*_*_*_*_*_*_*_*_*_*_

Thank you for taking the time to read my ebook.

Check out The Council (book 5):

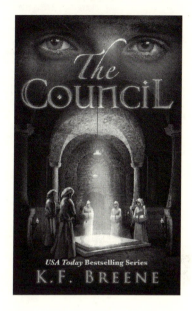

Never miss a new release or sale: http://eepurl.com/F3kmT

Website: Kfbreene.com
Facebook: www.facebook.com/authorKF
Fan and Social Group: https://goo.gl/KAgoNr
Twitter: @KFBreene

Review it. Please support the book and help others by telling them what you liked by reviewing on Amazon or Goodreads or other stores. If you do write a review, please send me an email to let me know (KFBreene@gmail.com) so I can thank you personally! Or visit me at http://www.kfbreene.com.

Lend it! All my books are lending-enabled. Please share with your friends.

Recommend it. If you think someone else might like this book, please help pass the title along to friends, readers' groups, or discussions.

THE COUNCIL (BOOK 5)

Sasha's journey continues in:

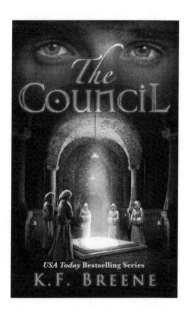

Chapter 1

"Sasha, hurry up. They'll leave without us!" Charles paced by the door, his knitting supplies in one hand and a horrible rendition of a quilt in the other. Scarves were something that the man could do. Blankets even came out decently, if he chose the colors correctly. An object half-crocheted and half-knitted, one square at a time, then strung together? Not attractive.

"Charles, they aren't going to leave without us. If they were that close, Jonas would be—"

I cut off as Jonas' burly shoulders appeared just beyond the doorway. The nasty puckers of skin from our battle with an extremely powerful demon were finally healing, three weeks after the event. Jonas had an attractive appearance, but his surly attitude and grim expression made a person stop taking notice and shuffle quickly out of his way.

"Were you under the impression that the schedule didn't apply to you, human?" The timbre in Jonas' deceptively calm voice hinted that if I didn't hurry, he'd grab me by the scruff of the neck and drag me down the hallway.

"Mage, Jonas. I believe you are supposed to call me ma—"

Jonas took a step into the room.

A nervous chuckle sounded right before I said, "Sorry! I'm coming, I'm coming!"

"I would make a sexual joke, but we gotta go," Charles said.

"Yes, leave talking and walking at the same time for the more experienced of us." I snatched up my backpack filled with travel items and slipped out the door. Jonas followed me.

"So, motorhomes, huh?" I asked as we made our way to the front of the mansion from where we'd basically travel eight hundred miles to an undisclosed location like a pack of gypsies in a caravan. While those of us going to the Council could fly, the powers that be—Stefan and Dominicous—

didn't want all that human interaction if it could be helped. Since it was drivable, *voilà*.

"You guys get a motorhome. Most everyone else has to sit in a stuffy car. So thanks for not letting me ride with you guys," Charles muttered as we descended stairs. "I have to ride with..." He flicked his head toward Jonas.

"You guys get along; what's the problem?" I asked.

Charles shook his head, not bothering to answer because Jonas was so close. Didn't matter—I was just poking the bear, anyway. Everyone in my crew got along with Jonas, but at the same time nobody did. He pretty much minded his own business (when he wasn't minding my business). He wasn't a wine-and-roses type of guy. I thought getting stabbed was *more* fun than trying to relax around him.

"Well, we're headed into shark-infested waters," I said as we descended another set of stairs. "I want as much time as possible beforehand to cuddle."

"Don't use 'the Boss' and 'cuddling' in the same sentence," Jonas growled behind me. "It is not the image he needs around his clan."

I rolled my eyes. "No one pays attention to me, anyway. Plus, what do they think he does: beat me over the head, grab my hair, and drag me to bed?"

"He *should* do that," Charles muttered. "It'd teach you some manners."

"God you guys are cranky today," I replied.

"We're headed to the snake pit," Charles said quietly. "Toa has gone over all this—what to expect. How are you *not* cranky?"

I got a thrill as we stepped out the front door. The cool night air greeted me. Two large, deluxe motorhomes hummed by the curb. A small fleet of luxury cars waited nearby. Stefan stood patiently beside the smaller of the motorhomes, speaking quietly with Dominicous, his breathtakingly handsome face shut down into a stern leader's mask. Toa stood by the other motorhome, which would transport a tied-up Trek and Andris, the prizes of battles past. Dominicous would claim ownership of the two since he was the reigning authoritative force. That sounded great to me. I had enough to worry about.

Toa had gone over the details of the Council. It was a collection of some of the oldest members of their race. They were intensely powerful men and women with hundreds of years of experience, limitless wealth, no end of creature comforts, and no real threat they cared to bother with. They were mostly high in power levels and attached to mages near the top of the power scheme. This snake pit was writhing with power plays, deceit, alliances and strategy, all greedy for power and bored with it at the same time.

It didn't sound like a wonderful retreat.

What was worse was that as the only black mage to walk through their gilded doors, I would be target number one. I could expect constant advances to steal my heart away from Stefan, kidnappings in order to swap blood and tie me in a blood link, and a steady stream of challenges.

No, they wouldn't be Parcheesi challenges. This was a warrior race and as the new kid on campus, a human, and sporting one of the highest power levels, I would draw the nay-sayers who wanted to prove I was a weak simpleton. How? By beating me senseless, of course.

Toa had stopped in his explanation at that point to pat me comfortingly on the back. They wouldn't kill me, he reassured me, because one thing they would not waste was a top-level power. If someone killed me, they would be killed and probably tortured to boot. So rest assured, I would at least live. I might be forcibly tied to a dozen people via sucking blood, which would drive Stefan into a mindless killing spree, but I would be alive.

It took everything I had not to literally punch Toa in the face. The guy just didn't have that social awareness that most people did.

"Oh look!" Charles exclaimed as we stepped down off the stoop.

Jen, witch-twin number one, and her three-year-old were weaving in and out of the monstrous warriors, making their way to me. As they passed by, all the fierce eyes and hard faces softened and smiles appeared. People bent down to get eye-level with little Aurora. The little girl preened, half-shy and half-excited to meet her towering playmates, any of which would drop what they were doing for a quick minute with a child.

I had never seen a group of people covet children so much as this group. It amazed me constantly. Even Stefan, an absolute hard-ass except behind closed doors, would get down low, put out his hands, and crack a smile if Aurora came to play. Jen might be human, and more than a little spacy and batty, but without exception if she brought her daughter, she was welcome anywhere in the mansion. She even had a whole mansion full of eager babysitters.

"Hi Aurora!" Charles exclaimed, bending down with his horribly ugly quilt. "Look what I made you."

"What is that?" Jen asked as they stepped up.

"A blanket!" Aurora giggled as she patted Charles on the arm in greeting. Charles was a favorite. He was the only one she was never shy with.

He swung her up and jiggled her around in his arms. Aurora's squeals of delight drew in everyone's eyes and evoked smiles. Jonas put out his hands next, his stern face melting like hot wax when she reached out to him. He flew her through the air like Superman, his laughter matching hers.

"Anyway," Jen said with a smile as she watched her daughter squealing in delight. "We just came to wish you farewell. The others couldn't make it in time, but they say good luck and stay safe."

I nodded, that thrill of danger raging through my stomach again. "Thanks. You guys going to keep coming to learn to use your magic?" I asked, digging my hands in my pockets.

"Yes. We're doing so well that we don't want to stop and lose traction. And the Boss said that Jameson will be running the mansion, so he'll keep an eye on us. No one messes with us, though. After Delilah kicked that kid in the balls when he tried the pheromones, everyone kind of lost interest. And that stuff doesn't really work now, anyway."

I nodded as Jonas set Aurora down. The pheromones worked on most people right away, but the longer a human hung out with that 'motivator', the less it worked. Apparently this was already known by everybody except me. No one ever thought to mention it to the silly human, it seemed.

Such was my life.

"Well, we should probably go. I'm making everyone late," I said to Jen.

Jen nodded at me and guided Aurora in front of her until Charles whisked her up again. "Are the shape-changer people going, too?" she asked.

"Yeah," I answered as I made my way to Stefan. "They're flying though. They have a truce with this clan, but everyone is so keyed up about this council meeting, and so eager to be the head dick, that—"

"Sasha!" Charles hissed, putting his big palms over Aurora's ears. "*Language!*"

"Sorry. But, yeah, we don't need people fighting before we even get to the Council. The two groups still don't exist peacefully."

"Okay, well... good luck! Stay safe!"

I nodded at Jen as I reached Stefan. The world melted away as his eyes delved into mine before glancing at Jonas and

Charles. After a silent exchange, he took my hand and guided me into the motorhome. As soon as the door was shut, he settled into the dining area with a sigh.

"Tell me again *why* we need a vehicle big enough for a family of eight?" I asked, settling in beside him.

"Because I'm the Boss."

"Didn't answer my question."

He smirked, moving his arm so I could lean against his rock-hard chest. After the motorhome waggled into the road, I asked, "How come you don't have more kids at the mansion? It seems like people love them around."

His fingers traced strands of my hair lightly. "When I was little, the mansion was attacked. It was more or less a routine situation—the neighboring clans often checked our defenses. Most of the kids were whisked away and sheltered, but two died. After that, we stopped allowing our children at the mansion unless in specific situations."

"But can't someone just attack the places where you *do* have children?"

"The only race interested in attacking us, at present, is our own. Since trouble reproducing is a species-wide trait, and losing even one child pushes us farther behind human populations, we don't cross that line."

"But—and I am just playing devil's advocate here—wouldn't that be a great way to thin down the opposing forces. The enemy?"

"Yes. And, in turn, a great way to thin down us, as a whole. It would soon be a contest of who could kill the others' young. There is no faster way to end our species altogether."

"Well, there *is* a faster way."

He quirked an eyebrow at me.

"Tell the humans you are showing up to take over."

A smile graced Stefan's full lips. "That is true."

We listened in silence to the rumble of the motor, the moving box swaying to one side or the other as we turned corners. After a while of quiet contemplation, Stefan still stroking my hair, he said, "When do you think you will conceive? Is that something we can try for soon?"

The spit got caught in my throat. "What was that?" I choked out.

His lips traced my ear lobe. His hot breath heated my skin as well as my body. "With you I would know it's one of my own. I can be sure I'm the father. I've always wanted to be a father. To see what traits I passed over to my child."

"Oh, you can be sure, can you? What if I'm waiting until you're asleep and taking in the sights of the house, so to speak?"

The answering chuckle was deep and dark. "I would know. And someone would be dead."

"Well, now is that fair?" I retorted in mock outrage. "What if I wanted to sow my wild oats?"

"Is there a point to this conversation?"

I threw him a glare.

He chuckled again. "What would you do if you heard I'd been with another woman? Tell me truly."

My gut tightened and my fists curled of their own accord. Jealousy bubbling into rage would probably elicit something extreme.

"Exactly," he whispered, trailing his lips down my neck. "We exist for each other, and are both too violent to suffer someone else touching what's ours."

"I don't know that I'm violent," I breathed, angling my head so he could kiss my collar bone. "I'm just a crazy bitch with a jealousy problem where you're concerned."

"However you define it."

After another moment of quiet, I said, "Stefan."

"Hmmm?"

"Is this council meeting going to be a shit show?"

With a small inhalation, Stefan leaned back against the seat and pulled me closer. "I'd be lying if I said no. You will be sought after. Someone will try to bend you to their will—and we have no idea who or how you will fit in their plans. Until we learn motives, it'll be hard to know how the attack will come, or when. It'll be harder to keep you protected.

"As for me, they'll try to send me away, worried I'll gain favor of one of the Council members. I have a high power level, I am excellent with a blade, smart and can be ruthless. Plus, I'm a good leader—I'll draw notice. Some favorable, some not."

"So, we'll be in the fight of our lives."

I got a squeeze. "Yes. From the first minute we step onto Council soil."

The breath tumbled out of my mouth in a sigh. "Well, at least we have a few people we can trust."

Stefan resumed stroking my hair. "And I hate to say it, but we have the shifters. They're tied to you, and you to me. I don't like your connection with them, but in this, I'll take any help I can get."

"Just say it—*I was wrong*. Three little words: *I was wrong*. Or go a step further—Tim and his crew stuck around and helped us defeat the demon instead of taking off like cowards. It's not so hard..."

I got another squeeze. "Don't push your luck."

I snickered and settled in tight against him. "Well, whatever you say, I'm glad they're coming. They're different; I'm different..."

"There are other humans at this place."

I scoffed. "They're pets. They don't hold any positions of power."

"True, I suppose. Our way of sticking our tongue out at

the majority of humans who keep us in the shadows. I wish it was different. It would make our situation easier."

"Something in my life easy? Yeah right."

"Careful, Toa's Doom's Day cloud is hovering over your head."

I laughed and lightly elbowed him. "Well, we'll just have to stick together, no matter what comes."

"There isn't any other way. Especially not with what *will* come."

Buy it now: The Council

ABOUT THE AUTHOR

K.F. Breene is a USA TODAY BESTSELLING author of the Darkness Series and Warrior Chronicles. She lives in wine country where over every rolling hill, or behind every cow, an evil sorcerer might be plotting his next villainous deed while holding a bottle of wine and brick of cheese. Her husband thinks she's cracked for wandering around, muttering about magic and swords. Her kids are on board with her fantastical imagination, except when the description of the monsters becomes too real.

She'll wait until they're older to tell them that monsters are real, and so is the magic to fight them. She wants them to sleep through the night, after all...

Never miss the next monster! Sign up here!

Join the reader group to chat with her personally: https://goo.gl/KAgoNr

Contact info:
kfbreene.com/
kfbreene@gmail.com

OTHER TITLES BY K.F. BREENE

<u>Fire and Ice Trilogy</u>
Born in Fire
Made in Fire
Fused in Fire

<u>Finding Paradise</u>
Fate of Perfection
Fate of Devotion

<u>Warrior Chronicles</u>
Chosen, Book 1
Hunted, Book 2
Shadow Lands, Book 3
Invasion, Book 4
Siege, Book 5
Overtaken, Book 6

<u>Darkness Series</u>
Into the Darkness, Novella 1
Braving the Elements, Novella 2
On a Razor's Edge, Novella 3
Demons, Novella 4

The Council, Novella 5

Shadow Watcher, Novella 6

Jonas, Novella 7

Charles, Novella 8

Never want to miss the latest? Sign up here!

Check out her website: kfbreene.com

Made in the USA
Columbia, SC
07 July 2025